Ashcroft Security Saving Lena

Ashcroft Security

Rose Nickol

Published by Rose Nickol, 2023.

ASHCROFT SECURITY SAVING LENA

First edition. May 13, 2023.

Copyright © 2023 Rose Nickol.

ISBN: 979-8223660705

Written by Rose Nickol.

Chapter One

Lena Scott walked nervously into the office of Ashcroft and Associates. This was her sixth interview this week and she had another one that afternoon. She was glad it was finally Friday and that she had no interviews scheduled for the weekend. She had been searching for a job for several weeks, ever since she had been let go from her job as a loan specialist at the bank.

Let go, the politically correct term for fired. The way her supervisor had put it to her was that she was released from her position. She still couldn't believe they had fired her. It hadn't even been her fault. Ms. Brighton, her supervisor, had been very kind to her for the few years she had worked there.

That totally changed after Franklin Franks II, the manager's son, was finished with her. She had broken her rule of never dating anyone she worked with—Frankie. A rule she had put in place when she was let go from her first job in banking. Frankie had been so convincing and charming, promising everything she wanted to hear. She hadn't had a clue as to what he was up to or capable of.

Lena wasn't naive. She knew the score. Franklin wasn't the first workplace romance she had been involved in. The other one had gone bad, too, and she had been released from that job also. Two jobs in banking in seven years and she was fired from both of them, for the same thing. That was why she was applying for a job in a security agency. She knew absolutely nothing about the security business, but she needed a change. Besides that, none of the interviews she'd had with people in the banking business had been promising.

Twenty-five interviews in four weeks and nothing, not one callback, nothing. Frankie promised to blackball her and he had. Most of the applications she put in were never responded to. She filled out applications day and night on the internet trying to find something. Anything. Her meager savings were almost gone, her car payment was overdue, and she had a box of ramen noodles in the cabinet. Desperate wasn't the word for it.

Steeling herself for another letdown, she knocked on the door that was simply labeled "Security," hoping it was the right place. She verified the address matched the one she had been given on the phone.

"Come," a deep male voice said from the other side of the door. Lena wondered what the body attached to that voice looked like. Probably nothing like what her imagination had thought up. No one looked that good. She heard a click and the door swung open. She walked into an empty office and stood there for a moment looking around. "Sit," the voice said again.

The picture in Lena's mind became clearer. He would be tall, very tall, and would have wide shoulders, an athlete's frame, maybe like a football player. A man that knew how to handle a woman.

She could also picture his girlfriend. He wouldn't be married. He would date a different woman every night and they all would be beautiful, tall, thin, long flowing hair, the opposite of Lena. Lena wasn't short at five feet six inches, but slim, no. She had a few extra pounds she needed to drop. Baby fat, her mother called it. She had tried to explain to her mother that most people lost their baby fat before they hit their thirties, but her mother didn't seem to hear her.

She looked around and didn't see anything but a small sofa against the wall. She sat on the very edge of the seat and nervously smoothed down her skirt.

The man in her mind would still tower over her, and he wouldn't care about those extra pounds.

There was nothing but the couch. No table, no magazines, nothing. She took a small mirror out of her bag and checked her makeup and hair. She sat nervously clenching and unclenching her hands, wishing she had thought to stick her e-reader in her purse.

She sat, purse in her lap, her hand fiddling with it for what she was sure seemed much longer than it actually was. After a few minutes she heard a knock at the door. She looked around and didn't see any other doors except the one she had come in. She wondered why the person who had invited her in wasn't answering the door.

The knocking continued incessantly until Lena couldn't take it anymore. She didn't even know if the door would open. Smoothing her skirt again as she stood, she walked over to the door and opened it a crack. "Security," was all she said.

"Is this the Ashcroft Security office?" The most amazing man stood on the other side of the door. He was tall, several inches taller than Lena, his big frame filling the doorway. His head almost reached the top of the door and his shoulders were so wide he could hardly fit through it. He looked like a weight lifter and it was all Lena could do to keep from drooling at him. It was as if the man from her imagination had come to life. He had dark brown hair and steel-gray eyes that looked as if they could see deep into her soul. A rugged face and strong chin. Not a classically handsome man, attractive in his own way. The look of someone who had seen the best and worst life had to offer. Lena wanted to sit him down and hear his life's story. It would be interesting, she was sure.

"Yes," she answered. "The owners are busy at the moment. I'm Lena. I'm waiting for an interview. Are you here on business?"

"Yes," the man answered and pushed his way into the room.

Lena wasn't sure what to do and stood watching the man as he made himself comfortable on the couch, right where she had been sitting.

The man patted the seat beside him, silently asking her to sit.

Lena looked around again, and seeing no other option other than standing there like an idiot, she sat on the edge of the couch smoothing her skirt again, a nervous habit she had acquired since she started going on so many interviews.

"So you're here for the receptionist position?" the man asked.

"Yes, I applied by e-mail and then did a phone interview with Mr. Ashcroft. This is my first time being here." Lena didn't know why she was volunteering so much information. She didn't know this man from Adam, but she felt very comfortable with him.

"So have you done this kind of thing before?" he asked.

"Kind of. I worked in banking for a long time, but I've done some receptionist work," she answered.

"Did you like it?" the man asked.

"Yeah, it was okay. I like getting to know people and greeting people and answering the phone isn't too hard," she answered, smiling.

"I guess it wouldn't be. Why the change? Why didn't you get another job in the banking industry?" the man asked, smiling back at her.

Lena thought a minute and decided to tell the truth. "The last two jobs I had didn't work out and I decided it was time for something different. I've been looking for a job for several weeks and haven't had any luck yet," she answered and it was all she could do to keep from bursting into tears. She really needed this job and she was about to give in and tell this stranger her life story. *She was pathetic.*

"Do you think you'll like working in the security field?"

This was starting to feel like an interview, Lena thought and wondered who this man was. Maybe it was time to start asking some questions of her own.

"I don't know. I don't know much about it. Are you here to hire them for something or for a job?" Lena asked, feeling a little braver.

"No, I'm Harold Klein. I came here to talk to the owners. You can call me Hal," he answered and lifted his hand to shake hers.

Lena shook his hand. It was so large it engulfed hers and she felt a little spark shoot up her arm as they touched. "Nice to meet you, Hal. If I get the position here, maybe I'll see you again."

"Oh, you can bet on it, honey," Hal answered and his low gravelly voice rumbled through her body.

Lena swallowed, her mouth suddenly dry. She wished she had a piece of gum or something, but that wouldn't be very professional.

Lena heard a sound and looked up to see a door she hadn't noticed before opening. As she looked closer, she noticed it was built into the wall in such a way that you wouldn't see it unless you knew it was there.

The man that walked out was gorgeous, even more so than Hal. He walked up to Hal and stretched out his hand. "Hal, great to see you again." He then turned to look at Lena. "Ms. Scott? I assume you're here for the interview?"

"Yes," Lena answered. "Are you Mr. Ashcroft?"

"No, I'm a partner of Mr. Ashcroft's. I'm R.J. Blackmore. If you'll have a seat, I'll be right back." He indicated the sofa and led Hal off to the office.

Lena relaxed against the sofa as she watched the two men disappear behind the door. She felt a shudder run through her body and had a feeling of impending doom, but didn't know what was wrong.

Chapter Two

R.J. led Hal into his office and closed the door. "Well, what did you think?" he asked as they sat.

"Why all the subterfuge? She's great, and beautiful. It was all I could do to keep my hands off of her. Her pictures don't do her justice. Did you listen?" Hal asked.

"Yeah, I heard it all. Mel wanted it set up this way. You know how he can be. You're right. She's so much more than her biography and photograph show and I agree, she's a sub, but may not know it. None of the history I got indicates she's ever been to a club or dabbled in the lifestyle, though her reading selection on her e-reader tells me she's interested enough in it. She has over a hundred romance books on the subject. She gave you the same answers Mel got over the phone. Did you read her background?"

"Yeah, girl's had a rough life. I don't think either of the positions she had before knew what they had."

"No, and I don't believe any of the stuff they tried to say about her. She just doesn't have it in her to do those things. I think she's a submissive and that's why those assholes were able to take advantage of her."

"Yes, I agree. Now we need to talk about how we're going to handle her latest problem. Did Mel say why his FBI contact asked us to investigate her?"

"Right. He just said that when he started the pre-employment investigation on her they were very interested in her and asked him to forward everything he found on her to them. Do you think she has a clue as to what's going on?"

"No, I don't. Let's get her out of here and see if we can get her talking, then we'll know more."

"Sounds good. How do you propose we do that?"

The men finished talking and made a plan then went out to whisk Lena off.

WITH EYE-CANDY LIKE that in the office it couldn't be too bad of a place to work, Lena thought. She just might like this. Hal was handsome in a rugged way, and R.J., wow. He was just wow. Blond hair just brushing the top of his collar. Ice-blue eyes. Handsome didn't describe him. He was what she pictured a Norse god might have looked like. She could picture women falling to their knees and worshipping at his feet. Yes, she was at the head of that line. She could think of at least one other thing she would do while on her knees in front of him. She'd slowly release his zipper. His cock would be so hard she would have to go slowly to keep from hurting him. Once she had him freed from the confines of his pants, she would try to wrap her hand around him, but he would be too large for her fingers to touch. Taking that beast into her mouth would take some work, but she could do it.

She let her mind continue to drift while she waited. What would it be like to have the attention of those men? In the few minutes she had been with them she had felt her body flush with heat, and parts she didn't know she possessed had been starting to wake up. She let herself imagine what they would be like in bed. Her mind was still wandering and when she heard the door open again, she felt herself flush. *Stop it,* she told herself, *they can't read your mind and have no idea what you were thinking. Smile, be professional. You need this job. Don't screw it up.* Mental talk completed, Lena stood awkwardly in front of the couch, not comfortable sitting down.

"It was good seeing you again, R.J. Call me soon and I'll bring you the numbers on that deal, but I think I can get my guys to go for it."

The man Lena had been talking to, Hal, slapped Mr. Blackmore on the back and let himself out the door. Just before he stepped out the door, he turned to Lena and winked.

Mr. Blackmore then turned to Lena. "Ms. Scott, follow me."

Lena glanced once more toward the door Hal had just walked out and followed R.J. into the office. She felt a little like Alice sliding down the rabbit hole, but she wasn't sure why.

"Have a seat, Ms. Scott." He indicated a leather chair placed in front of the massive desk, and Lena perched on the edge.

He started to ask the standard interview questions and Lena relaxed. At the end of the conversation, he offered Lena the job.

She gladly accepted and stood to shake his hand and leave.

"Ms. Scott..." he started.

"I think since we're going to be working together you can call me Lena, Mr. Blackmore," she stopped him with a smile.

"Lena, call me R.J. I was wondering if you would be willing to join Hal and myself for a drink, to celebrate, and I can fill you in more on what we'll expect from you around here. I'd like to tell you more about the business. What do you say?" he asked, a boyish grin on his face.

Oh, this is so not a good idea, Lena thought, as she nodded her head. *What could one drink with two gorgeous hunks hurt? That's all it was going to be just a drink or two to celebrate. Nothing more. She wasn't going to make the same mistake a third time.*

R.J. led Lena to a waiting car. Hal was already in the backseat. This shocked Lena a little. *Had they planned this?* She was beginning to doubt her decision. She slid in the middle of the seat, and R.J. slid in beside her. She felt a little trapped, squished between the two large men.

"I see you talked her into it," Hal said as she slid in.

"Yep, but I promised to talk business, so behave," R.J. answered with a chuckle. "Lena, Hal, Mel, and I were in the Navy together. We were all Navy SEALs and Hal was my dive partner. We've known each other for a long time. My meeting with Hal today was to firm up some business dealings. He's buying into the firm and you'll be working with him as much as you will be with me. You still need to meet with Melvin Ashcroft, the owner, who is out of state right now checking into some contracts. He'll be back sometime tomorrow. Don't worry, I have the authority to hire you. The job is yours. Mel respects my decision."

R.J. and Hal proceeded to tell her about the business and give her a hint of what her duties might be. Hal's arm rested along the back of the seat and his hand drifted down to cup her shoulder. Lena felt a shiver run through her body as Hal started casually rubbing his thumb back and forth over her collarbone. She glanced at that thumb out of the corner of her eye and wondered if the rumors were true, the size of a man's thumb was an indicator of the size of... She mentally shook her head, trying to clear her thoughts. She didn't need to be going down that path.

R.J.'s hand was lying on his leg, very close to her thigh.

A little too close for comfort. All he needed to do was to move that hand an inch and he would be touching her. This was way too close to her fantasy.

She wondered what Melvin Ashcroft would look like and if he would be as gorgeous as the two men she was sitting between. Could she handle working with three of the most incredible men she had ever seen? Even though she hadn't seen Melvin Ashcroft, she knew he would be just as hunky as his friends.

Sitting in the backseat, Lena couldn't tell where they were going, but it didn't take long to get there. The car stopped and R.J. opened his door before the driver could get out and open it for him.

"I've told you not to do that," Hal said, shaking his head. "Thurston gets upset if he doesn't get to do his duties."

"Sir," Thurston said as he held out an umbrella for R.J.

R.J. winked at the man and grabbed the umbrella with a muttered, "Thank you," as he reached back into the car to help Lena out. The clouds had been dark when they left the office, but Lena hadn't expected this. R.J. held the umbrella and pulled Lena close to his side, using his body to protect her from the wind-driven rain. Before they got to the door, Hal was close to her other side and she was again sandwiched between the two men.

Lena still couldn't tell where they were until they got into the building. She looked up and found herself in the lobby of a very posh-looking hotel.

Hal and R.J. led her to the elevators, keeping her sandwiched between them, and pushing her in the first available one. She felt and looked like a drowned cat. They were all three soaked despite the umbrellas and short walk to the doors of the building.

Lena again had the feeling she was falling down the rabbit hole and looked up to find herself crowded into the corner of the elevator, her back to the wall. Hal and R.J. were both facing her and she had the feeling that maybe she was going to get kissed when the doors opened and an older couple walked in. "Klein, Blackmore," the older man said, greeting the men, then seeing Lena, "Miss," and nodding to her before the door opened again and he escorted his companion off of the elevator.

Lena assumed they were going to a rooftop bar or something like that. Though she had never been in one of them she knew that many of the popular downtown Denver hotels had restaurants on the upper floors.

The ride was over fairly quickly and the men had turned around and were talking softly to each other. It was as if they had forgotten she was there. When the doors opened, instead of being in a bar or restaurant or hallway, they opened into a large living space.

Hal turned to her. "This is our penthouse apartment. You have to have the code to get to this floor so no one will bother us. I thought you might want to freshen up and get out of those wet clothes." He gently took her by the elbow and led her down a long hallway and through a large bedroom, to the largest bathroom she had ever seen. Her entire apartment would fit in the space. There was a glass-enclosed shower that her entire family would fit in. The sunken tub was just as large. All of the furnishings were marble and the fixtures were, Lena assumed, gold plated. The room looked more masculine than feminine and Lena wondered if the men's wives used this room or had one of their own.

"Feel free to use the tub or shower. I'll put towels on the bar to warm and see if I can find a robe or something for you to wear. Leave your clothes on the floor and I'll pick them up and have them cleaned when I bring the robe."

Lena thanked him and he left the room, closing the door behind him. She hadn't realized how wet and cold she was until she was left standing in the middle of the large room. Afternoon storms were not rare in the Denver area and she should have been better prepared. Even with the umbrella and the protection of the men's bodies, she was still soaked. She felt a blast of warmth and realize that Hal must have turned the heat on, since he and R.J. were soaked also.

She wasn't going to get warm standing there and although she looked at the tub with longing, she knew if she chanced it, she might be found sleeping and that would not be good. She started the shower to warm and began stripping her wet clothes off, folding them neatly and setting them on the edge of the vanity closest to the door. She was standing there in her bra and panties, which were also soaked and pretty much see through now, when the door opened a crack and Hal stuck his head in. "Oh, sorry," he said, quickly pulling his head back and sticking in one arm, a soft white terry cloth robe clutched in his hand.

Lena grabbed it and held it to her. "Thank you," she said softly, backing into a corner, holding the robe tightly as if to keep it from disappearing. The door closed and Lena crept up to it, looking to see if she could lock it. She locked the door then looked around for a towel. Crap, she thought, remembering Hal said he would put them on the warmer.

She unlocked the door, with reservations, but really wasn't worried about Hal or R.J. coming in except to bring towels. She hung the robe on the hook outside the glass shower door, hoping it would hide her from prying eyes if the door came open again.

Lena was standing under the warm spray of water when she thought she heard the door open again and let out a small scream. Then she heard Hal's voice saying, "To operate the shower there's a panel on your left. The top button..." He went on to explain all the different features. "I left warm towels on the vanity. Do you need anything else?" he asked.

Lena hunched over, trying to hide her body and make it as small as possible, and answered, "No, I'm good, thanks." Adding a mental, *Now stay out, please.*

Hal closed the door and walked out to the living room where R.J. was sitting on the couch, sipping a drink. Both men had changed and were lounging on the couch waiting for their prey.

"So how is our little mouse doing?" R.J. asked, leaning back comfortably. What they hadn't explained to Lena yet was that three of them, R.J., Hal, and Mel, shared not only the penthouse of the thirty story building, but women as well. They were very interested in sharing Lena, the little mouse that had crept into their office and hearts. Mel had seen it first when he investigated her after she applied for the receptionist position.

R.J. and Hal had been following and watching her for a week after they all read the reports Lance Lewis and his brothers, one team of field operatives that theyemployeed, had given them. They had been assigned to look deeper into Lena and find out why the girl had been unable to find a job. Franklin Franks, Lena's ex-boyfriend, had let her take the fall for his blunders. He was the son of the manager of the bank and all the loans he was in charge of were not what they appeared to be. When he had been caught, he had sold Lena out to cover his own ass. She was in deeper trouble than she realized.

Frank had not only sold her out to her employer, but also to some of his seedier associates and several of the unsavory contacts were out to extract payment from Lena for the funds Franklin owed them. Lena was unaware of any of it as far as they could tell. She had no idea who was after her and what kind of danger she was in.

Mel, Hal, and R.J. had had several meetings and decided the best way to keep her safe was to get as close to her as they could. They could have simply just told her what was going on, but they were afraid she wouldn't believe them and she would run. They couldn't have her out there somewhere alone and scared. She needed their protection. After watching her for several days, they were all eager to get closer to her and find out more about her.

Chapter Three

Lena finished her shower and felt much warmer. Grabbing the fluffy robe, she pulled it on. It was made for someone much larger than she was. She had to roll the sleeves up past her wrists to see her hands. She lifted the hem to keep from falling over it, and opened the door before she stepped out into the bedroom. She could hear the men's voices outside the room but decided to explore a little first. She turned to her left and walked down the short hallway to the first open door. This was definitely a man's room. She could tell by the darker, more muted colors and the sturdy heavy furniture. No signs of femininity in here. There were four more doors, all open, and she continued her explorations. The next room was also masculine, but in a different way—the colors were different, the furniture a different style, but still sturdy and heavy. The third room was the same. She thought she heard footsteps and darted back to the room at the end of the hall. It was the largest, with a huge bed, and several dressers lined up against one wall. The bed was the biggest she had ever seen and she could easily imagine several people sleeping in it.

She was just getting ready to step farther into the room to explore further when she felt a large warm masculine body come up behind her. "Oh!" she exclaimed, startled, giving a little jump. She felt the warm band of a male arm catch her under her breasts and save her from falling backward. She let herself lean into the warmth and strength for a brief minute before she straightened and turned her head to see who was behind her. "Hal, hi... I was just coming to find you," she said, her voice a little breathless at being caught.

Right. You went exploring, Hal thought to himself. "This is the largest bedroom," he told her before taking the arm he still had around her waist and turning her. Leading her to the first room, he stopped for a second in the doorway. "This is my room." He then turned to the two rooms, showing her which was Mel's and which was R.J.'s. "The three of us share this place. None of us are married or in committed relationships. We have a maid service that comes in twice a week and every now and then Mel's sister takes pity on us and cooks for us. Other than that we are just three old crabby bachelors."

"Speak for yourself. I refuse to be old, and crabby is a mean word. I prefer moody," R.J. said, walking up to them. "And don't fucking tell me moody is for women. I've seen your crabby ass be moody, too." He grabbed Lena's hand. "Come on, I'll show you the kitchen and balcony. We have a great view. You can see for miles."

Lena let him lead her through the chef's dream of a kitchen, admiring the stainless-steel appliances and granite countertops. What she wouldn't give to spend a few hours making a meal for them all there. She hadn't even met Melvin Ashcroft yet and could already imagine herself hanging out and spending time with all three of these men. *Stop it,* she told herself. She needed to get her head on straight. This was just a job and she couldn't afford to mess it up, again.

R.J. led her to the large balcony that overlooked the city and onto the plains. There was a huge hot tub, a table and chairs for lounging, and around the corner, a heated pool.

"This is perfect," Lena said, looking around in amazement. It was hard to tell she was thirty plus stories off the ground. The balcony looked like an outdoor oasis.

"We like to come out here and relax after being cooped up in the office all day," Hal said, walking up on the other side of her as she leaned against the rail around the balcony.

They were all three standing shoulder to shoulder against the rail looking out over the city. Lena took a deep breath. "I love the smell of the air after the rain," she said, leaning forward and looking at the small shapes on the street below. It was hard to tell now that it had been storming just a few minutes ago.

Hal grabbed her hand and pulled her back to the couch. "I think we promised you a drink," he said, pouring a shot of Jameson's in each glass.

Lena took hers and took a healthy swallow. Warmth and Dutch courage in one gulp. She relaxed back against the couch and crossed one leg over the other, showing a fair amount of skin as she did. She reached for the edge of the robe to cover herself and Hal grabbed her hand. "Leave it, I like the view."

Lena wasn't quite sure what to say so she took another swallow of her drink. Hal had been standing across the room and came to sit on the other side of her.

"So tell us more about yourself," he said, grabbing his drink and resting one arm along the back of the couch behind her.

"I sent your clothes down to be cleaned. They should be back shortly. Until then we can talk and relax here. When they get back we'd like to take you to dinner if you don't have any other plans," R.J. said from her other side.

"I need to make some calls. I had interviews scheduled for this afternoon, but I guess I don't need them now," Lena said with a sigh.

"No, honey, you have the job with us if you want it. We haven't discussed everything yet, but I think you'll like it," Hal said, letting his hand drift to her shoulder the same way it had in the back of the car.

R.J. stood and led her back to the big bedroom. "Here, honey, you can make your calls in here and come back to the living room with us when you are done. Are you hungry? We could order some snacks or sandwiches or something."

Lena nodded. She needed to eat. She hadn't had anything except coffee that morning and was starting to feel the effects of the alcohol she had. There was no place to sit in the room except on the bed, so Lena sat on the side of the bed to make her calls.

She made the calls she needed to, and let herself lie back on the bed, just for a minute. She hadn't been sleeping much between trying to do as many interviews as she could in a day and lying awake trying to figure out what she was going to do about paying her bills.

HAL WALKED BACK INTO the living room with a shit-eating grin on his face. R.J. looked at him. "What's up with you?"

"You should go sneak a peek. Our girl's back there sleeping and her robe slipped open," Hal answered, still grinning.

"You pervert. Why didn't you cover her up, asshole? I'll go do it." R.J. jumped up from the couch and headed back to the bedroom. Lena lay on her stomach on the bed. The robe had moved up to her midback, leaving her ass bare. She had one leg bent at the knee, leaving a very nice view. R.J. grabbed the throw that was on the end of the bed and unfolded it, placing it over her delectable ass. Lena stirred as he placed the blanket but settled immediately when he placed a soothing hand on her back and quietly whispered, "Shh, baby, go back to sleep. We'll take care of you." He couldn't resist bending down and brushing a soft kiss across her forehead. He stepped back to the foot of the bed and stood watching her a minute, feeling a bit like a voyeur, before he turned and walked back to the main room where Hal was waiting.

R.J. had poured them each a shot and Hal grabbed his, tossing it back. "Did you order some snacks?" he asked.

"I thought I'd let her nap a while then call, unless you want something while we call Mel and talk this over. We need to make a plan. This is going to be about more than just protecting her," R.J. said, walking over and getting his phone.

"You feel it, too?"

"Yeah, I think Mel did, too, after what he's said."

"Do you think she would go for what we want?" Hal asked, sitting in one of the big chairs on either side of the couch.

"Jeez, Hal, how would I fucking know that? You know as much about her as I do at this point. Damn, man, do you think I'm a fucking mind reader?"

"Shit, calm down. You know you're better at reading people than I am, that's all I was asking."

"We need to spend some time with her and see where if any place this goes. After the last two assholes she was with, I wouldn't blame her if she swore off men forever," R.J. said, wondering if they even had a chance.

Hal, Mel, and R.J. had all been friends for several years and had discovered that dating different women didn't work for them. R.J. didn't know if they were all a little damaged or just wired differently than the rest of the world, but they were happiest when they all three concentrated on a project together, whether that project was professional or personal.

Once they realized this and started dating women together they found their strengths and realized they each had something different to offer a woman. They complimented each other and where one of them was weak another was strong. There was no jealousy. They were a team working together and all three pieces fit.

Hal stood and walked back to the bedroom, pulling the door closed so that their conversation with Mel wouldn't wake their sleeping beauty. He hoped she would be theirs.

R.J. had Mel on the speakerphone when he walked back into the room. "Did you find out anything more about the people that are after her?" R.J. asked.

"From what Lance was able to find there is more than one group after her. Franklin Franks the second was involved with some very bad characters. He blamed everything on our girl and all the paper traces back to her. The Feds are involved and they want her for questioning. You know how those assholes can be. I've talked to my contact there and he's agreed to let me handle her for now. How long he can keep things quiet, I have no idea. What's your read on her?"

R.J. explained what had happened so far that afternoon and what his impression of Lena and her situation was. Hal added his views and the three discussed strategies for keeping Lena safe. They argued for several minutes about what she should be told about the trouble she was in and were still arguing when Hal saw her walking down the hall from the bedroom.

LENA WOKE TO THE SOUND of raised voices. She listened for a few minutes before she walked out to see what was going on. She couldn't have heard them right. It sounded like they were talking about protecting her and that she was in some sort of trouble.

Hey, did you have a nice nap?" he asked, walking over to her.

"Yeah, I heard you guys. Were you talking about me?" she asked. Maybe she hadn't heard them right.

Hal walked her back to the couch and once again she found herself sitting between the two men. "Lena, we are talking to Melvin Ashcroft, our partner and the man you interviewed with on the phone. I don't know how much or what you heard, but before you say anything the four of us need to talk."

Lena sat on the couch, wondering what she had gotten herself into now. Trouble seemed to find her no matter what she did. It was like she was a magnet for it.

"Hi, Lena. I know we've talked on the phone before. I'll be back tomorrow, but I don't feel we should wait until then to talk," the voice on the phone said.

Lena nodded, then realizing the voice couldn't see her, said, "Okay."

Mel went on to explain what was going on. Lena sat listening, her eyes wide. She couldn't quite process it all. "Wait, you mean all those loans I processed at Franklin's request were bad?" she asked, her voice full of doubt.

Hal placed one hand on her thigh and answered, "We are checking into them, but yes, a large number of them were not what they seemed."

Lena slapped at Hal's hand and shook her head. "I verified all the paperwork myself. Nothing was out of order. I checked everything thoroughly." She had no idea how she could have been fooled. She had been burned at the last job she had and she had been very careful. In the banking business all a person had was their reputation and it was very easily damaged.

"Why, why would you do this for me? You don't know me. I can't pay you. I can't even afford the rent on the craptastic apartment I have. You can't know how exciting it is to have to crawl over homeless people and fight off the drug dealers and pimps just to live in one room. My wonderful apartment, where I push the dresser in front of the door every night so no one walks in on me while I sleep. And now you tell me that someone is probably after me for helping that sniveling weasel of a man who called me sweetheart and said he loved me, while all the time he was screwing half the women in the accounting department," Lena finished with a sob. Where had she gone so wrong? All she had ever wanted was to make her own way and help people. She didn't think that was too much to ask.

When Lena started crying, Hal couldn't help himself and pulled her into his lap, holding her close and trying to soothe her. "Honey, we'll help you and you can stay here with us or we will put you up in a hotel. You never have to go back there if you don't want to," he said, holding her close and rocking her in his arms.

Lena sniffled and looked into his steel-gray eyes. "Why would you do that for me? You don't even know me." She couldn't understand the feelings she had for these men already and was afraid of making another mistake. She pushed off of Hal's lap and immediately felt the loss of contact but couldn't let herself give in to the feelings she had. That was why she was in this mess. She gave in too easily and trusted everything she was told. She needed to learn not to trust anyone but herself. She was the only person she had to depend on.

"Are my clothes back? I think I need to go home and think about some of this," Lena asked, looking around for her things.

"Hold on, Lena," the voice on the phone said. Lena had almost forgotten about Melvin Ashcroft, her new boss. "I think we need to talk some more. It's not safe for you to go back to your apartment alone. If you want to go and get some things, Hal and R.J. will go with you, but we don't want you going back there alone."

Lena really didn't want to go back to her apartment alone but wasn't sure she should listen to these men. "How do I know I can trust you and no one told me who's going to pay for all this."

R.J. pulled a file folder out of his briefcase that was beside the couch and laid it in front of Lena. He flipped it open and the first picture was of her and Simon, the man she had been dating at her first banking job. "Lena, do you know who this is?" he asked.

"That's Simon. He was the manager over the loan department at the first bank I worked for. I went out with him a couple times."

The next picture was of her and Simon at his father's mountain cabin, skiing. There were several more of her and Simon, then several of her and her best friend Trina. The last few pictures were of her and Frankie. Someone had been following her for months. "How long have you been watching me?" she asked, starting to shake.

R.J. slid one arm around her and pulled her to his side. "Relax, honey, we haven't been on the case that long, someone else took the pictures of you before we started."

"Who, who's been watching me? Why were they taking pictures of me? Some of these pictures go back several years." Lena was starting to panic. Hal, Mel, and R.J. knew they had to do something to calm her down before she went into a full-blown anxiety attack.

Mel quickly decided the best way would be to tell her the truth and put all his cards on the table. It would be better to be able to talk to her in person, but there was no way to do that right now. He couldn't let her work herself up all night. He had to tell her at least part of what was going on.

R.J., Hal, and Mel had worked together long enough that R.J. and Hal knew what Mel was going to do and prepared themselves to handle the fallout. They hoped they could keep Lena calm enough to keep her from running screaming and never talking to any of them again.

"Lena, you need to know that the FBI has been watching you for a long time. They were watching Simon and the bank before you started working there. After Simon realized he could keep up his illegal activities but pin the blame on you, he got even deeper involved in the criminal world. How he and Franklin Frank II are involved we aren't sure yet, but we are sure they are. They both travel in the same circles and have several of the same contacts."

"I'm being watched by the FBI. Am I going to go to jail?" Lena put her hands over her face. What was she going to do?

"Lena, don't worry about it, honey. We'll be here to help you. Nobody's going to put you in jail. From now on one of us will always be with you," Hal told her as he pulled her into his arms. He knew they were rushing things, but he couldn't help it, he had to touch her.

Lena was so confused and overwhelmed. "Am I safe going home? You probably know my apartment isn't in the best of neighborhoods. I never really felt very safe there anyway." Lena quickly thought of places she could go. She couldn't afford to get a hotel. Maybe she should call Trina. Then she thought what if she got Trina or someone else hurt. What was she going to do?

R.J. could see the panic on her face. He reached over and pulled one of her hands down and held it between his own.

Hal wrapped his arms tighter around her and they both tried to reassure her everything would work out.

"Lena, I know you don't know us very well, but please trust me and my friends. We'll do our best to keep you safe. We want to find out who is doing this and why."

"Why would you want to help me? You don't even know me." Lena let herself relax onto Hal's lap. She knew she shouldn't but for some reason she felt safe with these men and in her heart she knew they would do as they promised.

"Lena, I'm working with my contacts in the FBI to find out what is going on and why they picked you to take the fall for all of this. It could be you were just a nice woman in the wrong place at the right time for them to take advantage of," Mel told her. He hoped what he was saying was true and that she wasn't involved in all of this. From what they had been able to determine she had just got caught up in something she didn't understand, but the FBI wasn't sure that she wasn't involved. It would be all he could do to keep them from taking her into custody and questioning her. He was pretty sure she didn't know anything. If she did know something, she wasn't aware of it. They would have to tread carefully with her.

Lena realized she was still sitting in Hal's lap and her robe had flapped open, leaving a fair amount of cleavage and leg showing. Pulling her hand away from R.J., she pulled the edges of the robe together and pushed herself away from Hal, getting to her feet. "Are my clothes ready yet?" she asked, pulling her robe so the edges overlapped and walking a couple steps away. She needed to get out of there and figure out what she was going to do. She couldn't think straight around them.

She looked around for her phone and remembered she had left it in the bedroom. "I really need my clothes," she told them again as she walked back to the bedroom to find her phone.

She found her phone on the bed and sat to make her calls. She sat looking at her phone for a few minutes, trying to decide who to call. Trina was pretty much her only friend, but she didn't want her to be involved in anything that could get her hurt. She could call her parents or her brother. Her parents would help her but her dad would tell her what a failure she was and how she should have gone into the family business of farming and stayed to help him like her brother did. Her brother would tell her about how since she had to go off and live in the city he had had to stay and help with the farm. A bunch of guilt she didn't need. They had given her enough when they learned she had lost her first job. She hadn't even told them about losing her last job. She was determined to make it on her own.

Lena put her phone down and started crying. She wasn't a failure but felt like it in this moment. After crying for a few minutes she looked up and saw R.J. and Hal standing in the doorway looking at her.

Hal held her clothes in his hand. "Thurston just brought these up. He'll take you wherever you want to go...but we'd really like you to stay here or let us put you up in a hotel until all this calms down and we find out for sure what is going on. All we want is to keep you safe and we feel we could do that better if you were here with us."

"But we understand if you're not comfortable with that," R.J. added quickly.

Both men looked very contrite and Lena felt a little sorry for worrying them so much. "Do you really think I'm in danger? Nothing has happened so far," she said, biting her lip.

Hal walked into the room and sat on the bed beside her. "We can't be sure, but until we figure out how Simon and Frank are connected and exactly what they were doing, I don't think you will be safe. The FBI has been watching both of them for years but hasn't had enough evidence to do anything. They have someone undercover in both banks trying to make connections, and hopefully will have something soon."

"So what am I supposed to do in the meantime? Put my life on hold and hide, like a scared rabbit? I refuse to do that and I refuse to put the people I care about in harm's way. There has to be a way out of this." Lena was so confused and tired. She didn't think she had ever been so tired in her life.

"If I stay here, I can have my own room and you won't—" She paused, trying to think of a nice way to say *take advantage of me*. "You won't try anything and I'll just be your house guest."

"Lena, nothing will happen that you don't want to. Nobody stays in this room. We each have our own rooms. You won't be putting anyone out by staying here. You can stay here as long as you want to," Hal said, a look of relief on his face. He had thought they were going to have a bigger battle with her and all he wanted was to see her safe.

"Here are your clothes. Get dressed and we will take you to your apartment to get anything you might need to stay here for a few days," R. J. told her, handing her the clothes.

Lena nodded and absently took the clothes out of his hand. She really didn't have a better plan and if what they said was true she needed some place safe.

Chapter Four

R.J. couldn't believe the neighborhood Lena lived in. The building was dilapidated and looked ready to fall down. There were people sitting outside her building begging and trash everywhere. Lena smiled and greeted some of them by name, stepping over trash and debris. She cheerfully led them through the lobby of the building where others were loitering while children played.

"I thought this building was safer because you had to have a key to get into it. I found out about a week after I moved here that that wasn't true and the lock on the door didn't work. When I called management to complain about it they said they would look into it, but nothing ever happened. After I called five or six times with the same result, I gave up. Most of the people here are nice and I haven't had any trouble," she said, guiding them through the maze of humanity and furniture in the stair and hallways. She didn't want to tell them about people trying to get into her apartment at night. They didn't need to know that. "It wasn't this bad when I looked at it and I was going to move when my lease was up, but I can't afford it now." She didn't want to tell them about the parties and the drug deals in the stairwells. That would really freak them out, she thought.

She stopped and reached to unlock the door in front of them. Hal stepped in front of her and opened the door. It was like walking into a different world. Gone were the gloomy, dark hallways, the chipped and fading paint. It was like walking into a different universe.

She had painted the room a bright sunny yellow, and there were cheerful curtains and a vibrant throw over the couch. The room was small and very clean. She had placed colorful screens to portion off the room into separate areas for cooking, sleeping, and resting. It should have looked cramped and crowded, but her use of color and the arrangement of the furnishings made it look comfy and cozy.

Lena ducked around him and led the way into her home. She waved her arm to indicate they could sit on the couch. "Let me get a bag and I'll grab some things," she said, walking into the room and heading for the back corner. Soon they heard things rustling and she was back within a few minutes. "That will do for a few days. I just need to set up the plants. They all have self-watering pots so they will be okay for a few days. I have just a few more things to do. Do you want something to drink while you wait? Should we take something out to Thurston?" Lena asked as she continued gathering things. Thurston had decided to stay with the car. He had taken one look around and pulled a gun out of the glove compartment and laid it on the seat beside him. This seemed to strike R.J. and Hal as funny, and they both teased the man as they helped her out of the car. All Thurston said was, "Just in case, sir," then picked up his newspaper and started reading.

"Thurston will be fine, honey, and so will we. You just do what you need to so we can get to dinner," Hal told her, grabbing her e-reader off the table and turning it on.

Lena was intent on doing what she needed and didn't notice that Hal and R.J. were looking at her e-reader until she went to look for it to pack it. "Where's my..." she started to ask halfway to herself, when she noticed the men had their heads together and were looking at something. She walked around the couch to see what they were looking at. Her eyes got wide when she saw what they were doin. She immediately went into a panic. She had all her erotic romances on there. She didn't need them seeing that. How long had they been looking at it? They really didn't need to know her reading habits. Trying to be casual, she walked over to them and said, "Hey, I'm ready. I just need to find my...oh, there it is. My e-reader, I need to pack that." She reached for it.

"Not so fast, I'm reading something," R.J. said as he started reading out loud, "*Then he pulled Samantha facedown over his lap, adjusting her so that her bare pussy—*"

Lena grabbed for the device. "Give me that…I…I. Please don't read any more out loud," she pleaded when Hal captured her hand with his and pulled her down to sit on his lap. Lena tried to hide her face when R.J. moved it to his other side and continued reading.

"*Her bare pussy was wet and ready, waiting for him and his brothers.*"

"Oh, please, please stop reading," Lena pleaded. If she could disappear she would. She was more likely to die of embarrassment before that happened, though.

"Hold on, this is the good part," R.J. said as he once again continued the story. "Stop interrupting. Okay, remember Samantha is facedown over Jared's lap and her pussy is bare."

"Yeah, we got that part. Go on," Hal told him impatiently.

Lena turned her face into Hal's shoulder. How much more embarrassed could she get?

"*Before they could have their fun, Jared, Jake, and Jordan had a punishment to administer. Samantha had earned a spanking with her rude behavior and that was something they would not tolerate. Jared rubbed his hand over Samantha's bare ass cheeks, rubbing soothing circles over her lush bottom. It was full and round, nicely cushioned just as he and his brothers liked. He couldn't wait for them all to take her. He would take that virgin pussy while his brother Jake took her round little hole. They would have to be careful and prepare her. Samantha hadn't had many experiences with men and never with men like the three of them.*"

R.J. stopped reading and laid the device down. "Nice choice of reading material, darling."

"If you're done, can you go now?" Lena asked. She just wanted them gone. At this point she didn't care if she ever saw them again.

Hal cupped her face with both of his hands. "Don't be embarrassed about your choice of reading material. It says a lot about you and the kind of woman you are," he said, smiling.

Yeah, it shows what kind of pervert I am, she thought.

As if he could read her thoughts, R.J. said, "Don't be ashamed of your feelings or of who you are. Everyone has their own kink, and there are more poly couples than you think."

"There are? So this kind of thing isn't weird or something the author made up just to sell books?" she asked, relaxing a little. When she read her books they took her to another world where she could be a woman loved by one or more men and not shamed for her desires. "Is the spanking part real, too?" She was a little embarrassed asking the question but really wanted to know. When she had asked Simon or Frankie to spank her they had looked at her like she was crazy and she was so ashamed she never would talk with them about it again.

"Yes, darling. If you were ours you would be spanked and probably often," R.J. answered.

"Yours? You mean you two share women?" Her day was looking much brighter now. She wasn't thinking about her rule of not dating anyone she worked with and how her last two experiences had turned out. She was thinking about what it would be like to be between these two men and the wicked things they would do to her body.

Hal spoke this time. "Baby, not only do R.J. and I share, but Mel joins in also. The three of us share women just like the brothers in your book."

"Let me get this right. If I were interested in the three of you and you were interested in me, all three of you would share me. You would expect me to be enough for all of you." Lena was aroused at the thought of lying with the three of them and she hadn't even met Melvin Ashcroft yet.

"Mel, Hal, and I have shared the same woman before. Right now we're not seeing anybody, but that could change very soon," R.J.

answered, taking her chin and turning her away from Hal. He leaned in and brushed her lips with his very gently. "Think you're up to the three of us, darling?" he asked, deepening the kiss.

When he broke the kiss, Lena asked, "The three of you would want to date me and well...the other stuff, too?" Lena couldn't quite grasp what he was trying to tell her.

"Yes, we would want to date you, and if by other stuff you mean spank you, take care of your every want and need, and take you in every way a man can take a woman, then yes, that's what we mean," Hal answered.

"Think about it, Lena. Your body trapped between ours. One of us in your lovely little mouth, one buried balls-deep in that tight pussy of yours, and then there's the third one. He'd have to bury his cock deep in your ass. We would all take you together, bringing you so much pleasure you couldn't be sure your body could survive it. You would no sooner finish one orgasm than one of us would be giving you another. You would come in ways you never have before. After being with the three of us you would be spoiled for any other man. You would be ours forever." R.J.'s voice was deep and smooth, like the finest chocolate.

Just the thought of what they were proposing was causing Lena's body to tingle and she could feel the moisture gathering between her legs. What would it be like with the three of them? Could they do what they promised? "Punishment, you said something about being punished?" she asked, wondering if she was really considering this.

"Yes, darling, you would be punished. When you were bratty or mouthed off to one of us, we would flip you over our knee and bare that beautiful round ass and spank it until it was hot and red. If you were a good girl and took your punishment with class and dignity, we would reward you for good behavior," R. J answered.

"But we would never punish you unless you knew the rules. We don't want to hurt you and this is for you as much as it is for us," Hal put in quickly. He wanted to make sure she knew they weren't abusive.

"All three of you do this, Mr. Ashcroft, too?" It felt weird to be talking about doing something like this with someone she hadn't even met. She'd just talked to Melvin Ashcroft over the phone but if he looked anything like he sounded, he would be as amazing as his two friends.

"Yes, sweetheart, Mel likes the same things we do. That's what makes it easy for all three of us to share," R.J. answered.

"Do you think he will like me, too? I mean...I think...I... Do you like me?" God, she was making a fool of herself. She should just shut up.

"Yes, Lena, R.J. and I like you very much. We know Mel will like you. He's talked to you on your phone and he's seen pictures of you. Mel already likes you. He can't wait to meet you."

"I guess I can't wait to meet him either. So, say I wanted to try this thing, what would happen next?" Lena couldn't believe she was really thinking of doing what she was talking about with three men, one of whom she'd never met.

"Mel will be back tomorrow. Why don't you take until then to think about it?" R.J. suggested, taking a deep breath and wishing he could just fuck her and get it over with. He was going to have a problem sleeping tonight with the boner he had.

What the hell was R.J. doing? Hal couldn't believe his friend, pal, and, for all practical purposes, brother, was telling the soft warm bundle of woman that was currently sitting on his lap, rubbing that delectable ass against his rock-hard cock, that they would wait until tomorrow and she could take all night to think about being with the three of them.

He wanted her now. He couldn't even wait to get to the penthouse to take her. If he could he would take her right here. As usual R.J. was being the practical one. He was the one that kept the other two from going off the deep end. There had been lots of times that if not for R.J., Hal or Mel would be in jail or dead right now. R.J. was the voice of reason. And right now Hal didn't like it at all. Mel wouldn't either if he was there.

R.J. recognized the look Hal was giving him and gave him his *I don't give a shit what you think* look back. They were going to give Lena some time to think this over and let her at least meet Mel before they started something with her. They'd known the woman all of four hours and he was not going to let her rush into something.

"Honey, if you have everything you need for a few days, I'm sure Thurston has finished his paper and coffee by now and is ready to leave. Let's go get something to eat, then we will take you back to the penthouse and we can all try to rest for the night." He knew he wouldn't be getting any rest and by the look on Hal's face he was in the same condition.

R.J. stood and handed Lena her e-reader, and then grasped her hand and helped her to stand up.

Hal stood and quickly adjusted his pants and shot R.J. another dirty look before putting a more pleasant look on his face and sliding one arm around Lena's waist. R.J. may have given her the night to think things over, but if she snuck in his room during the night he wasn't going to send her away.

Dinner was nice. The men told Lena stories of their days with the SEALs and how they all met and were on the same swim team together. She laughed and enjoyed getting to know them better. It was over too soon and they all went back to the penthouse. It was too early to go to bed. Although they all wanted the same thing Lena wasn't going to start something with two-thirds of the trio. It didn't feel right for her to do that.

They got back to the penthouse and Hal took Lena's things back to the big bedroom. "This will be yours for as long as you stay with us," he told her, setting her things down and standing in the doorway.

"Thanks. Umm, which room is yours?" she asked. She wasn't sure she knew why she was asking but she wasn't ready for him to leave the room.

"The second one on the left, R. J. has the first one and Mel's is across the hall," he explained, using his hand to indicate the doors.

There was one more door that was closed and when Lena had tried the knob earlier when she was exploring it was locked. She figured it was a guest room or something but didn't ask.

Hal took a couple steps toward her and asked in a deep voice, dripping with sex, "Why did you want to know, baby? Should I leave my door open tonight and expect a visitor?"

Just as he finished his question, R.J. walked into the room. "What's keeping you two so long? I thought we might play some cards. It's too early to call it a night. Come on, it's Friday night," he said, pushing Hal out of the way and grabbing Lena's hand.

Hal gave him a dirty look and wondered if Mel would help him hide R.J.'s body. He would kill him quickly. He knew several ways to kill a man and not make a mess. R.J. deserved that. Surely Mel would understand. Heck, Mel would do the same thing in his place.

He heard Lena giggle and hurried out to see what R.J. was up to with their woman. He wasn't jealous exactly. He just wanted to make sure he didn't miss anything.

When he got out to the dining room, R.J. had Lena sitting at the table and he was explaining the rules of poker to her. Hal grabbed a beer for him and R.J. and poured Lena a glass of wine.

"So do we use money or what?" Lena was asking as Hal sat down and handed them each their drinks.

"For the first couple of games we'll use matchsticks and once you get the hang of it we will make it more interesting," R.J. told her, putting a pile of matchsticks in front of each of them.

Hal could just imagine ways to make things more interesting. He was so focused on the mental picture of Lena sitting there handing them an article of clothing for each hand she lost, that he lost the first game to her. It was worth it to see her clap her hands and bounce in her seat. He couldn't take his eyes off her breasts as she bounced and wondered if her nipples would be the same rosy brown color as her lips or if they would be a dusty pink. He couldn't wait to find out.

Lena saw Hal staring at her breasts and noticed that he wasn't paying much attention to his cards. She watched R.J. while trying to play the next hand and noticed he paid more attention to her than his cards. She put her cards facedown on the table and stretched, watching both men's faces as she did. Yep, they were watching her. She took a drink of her wine and wondered if she could add a little fun to the game.

She picked up her cards and looked at them again before making her bet and laying them back down. "It's warm in here," she announced, reaching for the buttons on her blouse. She undid the first couple buttons, leaving a good glimpse of cleavage before picking her cards up again.

She noticed Hal lick his lips, and then he made what she considered a stupid move. Hmm, maybe her plan would work.

They played a couple more hands, and Lena lost her first hand. Time to bring out the big guns. She gave a little groan and moaned, "Oh, a charley horse in my calf. Can I lay my leg across your lap, Hal?" Hal was sitting closest to her at the side of the table.

"Sure, darling, let me try and rub it out for you." It hadn't taken Hal long to figure out what Lena was doing and he wondered how far she was willing to go.

Lena slipped her shoe off and slid her stocking-covered foot into Hal's lap. She felt one of his hands grasp around her calf and start to rub. "Ohh, that feels, umm," she moaned, wiggling her foot a little.

Hal ran his hand up her leg to cup the back of her knee—he knew that was a trigger point for some women—and ran one finger through the crease. His action had the desired effect and Lena arched her leg, the heel of her foot rubbing delightfully against his bulging cock. If he got much harder he would burst, but he wasn't going to give in yet. R.J. may have given her until tomorrow to make her decision, but if she decided early he was sure Mel wouldn't mind if he and R.J. had a little sample. All he wanted was a little taste.

Lena lost that hand and the next. When she tried to move her foot, Hal held it in place with an evil grin on his face. Two could play at this game.

R.J. stood. "Hal, join me in the living room. I think we need to order some snacks. It looks like we might be playing a while."

Hal reluctantly put Lena's foot down and stood to follow his friend.

"I see what you are doing. Where do you think you are going with this?" R.J. asked, talking in a low voice and watching over Hal's shoulder to make sure Lena wasn't listening.

"I'm going the same place you want to. Come on, man, you know you want her as bad as I do. Mel won't care if we have a little sample. He can join us tomorrow."

"You can't wait one more day. We just met her." R.J. tried to be logical.

"Honestly, do you want to wait?" Hal looked his longtime friend in the eyes.

"Honestly, no I don't, but..." R.J. answered with a sigh.

"Then why should we. We'll just play a little." Hal started smiling when R.J. nodded.

"I'm going to go change into something more comfortable while you guys order snacks," Lena called out and darted down the hall to her room, hoping she had packed some of her sexier nightwear. There was more than one way to win a card game and get her way. Time to up the ante again.

Lena dug through her suitcase until she found it. "Perfect," she exclaimed and quickly changed. She ducked into the bathroom and quickly ran a brush through her hair, applying a little blush and lip gloss. She heard a knock at the door and skipped down the hall. She was going to be in so much trouble.

When the snacks arrived, Hal set the food out on the table and moved R.J. to the seat opposite him. They planned on crowding their girl a little. If she reacted like they thought she would, he would be getting more than his taste tonight.

R.J., control freak that he was, had texted Mel their plan, "just to make sure."

Hal topped off their drinks and took his seat at the table to wait on the others. While he was waiting he thought about Lena and the mess she was in. Due to the actions of the men she had been involved with, there were several individuals looking for her. He was surprised they hadn't found her in the seedy neighborhood she lived in, but maybe that was a good thing. Franklin Franks and Simon Bates had both been using bank funds to further their own career, while feeding Lena to the birds. He was sure she had no idea what had been going on. Bates had been known to use the internet to create false identities. Using these identities, he would take out small loans to cover his gambling debts. Once he found out he could create a side business of doing this and sell these loans to his gambling friends, he pulled Lena in, feeding the loans through her and removing his name from the contracts so that nothing traced back to him.

Franklin Franks II was doing the same thing. The Feds thought it was suspicious that Lena was involved in the duplicate activities at both banks and were sure she was the root of the problem. Mel, Hal, and R.J. felt differently.

Hal was still pondering Lena's problem when R.J. walked in and took his seat. "Did Dad give his permission?" he asked sarcastically.

"Yes, Mel gave his blessing. He can't wait to get home tomorrow and is going to try and catch an earlier flight. If he can get on earlier, he'll be here before noon."

"Good, I hope we let her out of bed by then," Hal said, laughing.

Lena came walking, sauntering was more like it, in the room and both men's mouths fell open.

Perfect. Just the reaction she had wanted. She had changed into a light blue satin pajama set. There was a long-sleeved jacket, which she had left unbuttoned over a camisole top. The top was V cut and left a lot of cleavage showing. It was also short and about three inches of her bare stomach showed above the loose fitting harem-style pants. Her feet were bare. Neither man could take their eyes off of her. She had left her long mahogany hair down and softly tousled.

She trailed her fingers across first R.J.'s back then Hal's as she seemed to float around the table before sitting down. She reached for her glass of wine and took a healthy swallow. She'd never tried to seduce one man, let alone two at once before, and needed a little Dutch courage.

"So, boys, what's the game? I'm tired of matchsticks, let's make it more interesting. Any suggestions?" she asked, her voice low and sensuous.

Shit, Hal thought, she was playing right into their hands, or were they playing into hers? The evening was about to get very interesting. He grabbed himself and R.J. another beer but vowed to take it easy. He was going to need all his facilities tonight or he would be the one naked on the table instead of Lena.

"Well, darling, we can make it as interesting as you want. What do you say to a little strip poker?"

Lena assessed each man, mentally calculating how many articles of clothing they were wearing and wished she had added a couple more pieces to her ensemble. "Sounds like fun," she answered, hoping she wasn't stepping in it.

R.J. explained how it was going to work and dealt the first hand. Lena lost her earrings. On the second hand Hal lost his shirt. After the sixth hand, by which both men were shirtless and Lena had lost her watch, they took a break to refill the drinks and get more snacks. Lena stepped back to the restroom and the men decided while she was gone that this was not happening fast enough. With R.J. keeping watch, Hal quickly stacked the deck. Time for Lena to lose her jacket.

Lena came back from the bathroom and took her seat. She lost the next two hands, leaving her sitting at the table in her camisole top and a very tiny pair of blue bikini panties. When she lost the third hand and all she had left to give was her top or her panties, she protested. "This isn't fair."

"Why isn't it fair, darling? We both took our shoes and socks off at the beginning of the game to even the odds, and we let you count your jewelry, which we didn't have to. You can either give up an article of clothing or go to bed," Hal said, smirking at her.

Lena thought a minute then she got an idea. "What if instead of an article of clothing I give the winner a kiss?"

"Give us a minute to talk this over," R.J. answered. He and Hal stood and walked into the living room.

They returned in a couple minutes and both had big smiles on their faces.

Lena wasn't surprised she was losing. When Hal had lost his first hand and took his shirt off, she couldn't stop her mouth from watering. When R.J. lost his shirt two hands later, it was all she could do to keep from drooling. She was looking at them more than she was looking at her cards and had made several stupid mistakes.

Both men agreed to accept kisses instead of clothes for the next couple of hands. The cards were dealt and Lena looked at her hand. Nothing. She tried to bluff her way through it, but still lost.

R.J. was the winner and sat triumphantly awaiting his prize.

Lena walked over to him and leaned down, placing a soft chaste kiss on his lips. She was a little disappointed when he didn't ask for more.

As she took her seat, she missed the look Hal gave R.J. If he had won the hand he sure wouldn't have let her off so easy. He stood and stripped off his jeans, standing there in a pair of white boxer shorts which did little to hide his erection. Lena's mouth gaped open a little more and she quickly averted her eyes.

It was Hal's turn to deal and he watched as Lena's eyes lit up as she looked at each card. He would have to tell her later she was not very good at bluffing. Her eyes were very revealing and he instantly knew if she had a good or bad hand.

Lena won the next hand and Hal walked over, lifting her to her feet. His turn to give the kiss. Threading one hand through her hair, he held her head in place and lowered his mouth to hers. He gently pressed his lips to hers and held them there for a few seconds. She looked so disappointed when he let her go it was all he could do not to grab her again and kiss her like he wanted to.

Lena dealt the next hand. She was still wearing her camisole and thong. Hal and R.J. were both down to briefs. This was going to be a very interesting hand. Lena picked up her cards and her face fell. She obviously did not have a good hand. Both Hal and R.J. were grinning like fools.

Lena put her cards down and reached for the hem of her top.

They could tell she was reluctant but gave her a minute to see what she would do.

As the winner of the hand, Hal felt he had the right to pick his prize. "Oh no, baby, over here," he said, beckoning her with one curled finger. He pushed himself away from the table and turned his chair, giving her room between him and the table. Reaching out with both hands, he clasped her hips gently and pulled her to him. "Straddle me." His voice was dark and gravelly. His eyes never left hers.

R.J. stood and came to stand behind Hal. R.J. hoped he knew where this was going. He and Hal had worked out a tentative plan but not detailed. He would just have to wait and see where Hal went with it.

He also kept his eyes on Lena, watching the rise and fall of her chest as her breath became rapid. The way the pupils of her eyes dilated. The graceful way she rose and stood proudly. He could see the small battle she had within herself as she made the two steps it took her to stand between Hal and the table. He knew the minute they won the battle.

He loved to watch the eyes of a submissive. He could always see the battles they had within themselves and relished the minute they decided to give, submit their body to him and his partners. She would be theirs. For how long, he didn't know.

Lena released her top and stood. With a quick glance to R.J. before walking to stand in front of Hal, for a moment she considered turning and running to her room. She could hide in there. Hal and R.J. had made it plain that she had the power to stop whatever this was whenever she wanted to. They would not push her, not pursue her. She could start work on Monday as if nothing had happened. Just three people getting to know one another and playing cards. Nothing more.

But she wanted more. For once in her life, she wanted to be the bad girl, the girl who had it all. She wanted her cake and to eat it, too. She didn't know if she would have the same chemistry with Melvin Ashcroft as she did with these two men, but he wasn't here and they were. They were hers, for tonight at least.

Lena let Hal pull her toward him and sat sideways on the edge of his knees. She looked over his shoulder and saw R.J. standing there naked. Her eyes grew wider as she stared at his erection. Wow, what they said about proportions was totally untrue. She couldn't help staring. It was long and hard, an angry red color and pointed right at her. "That looks like it hurts," she said, her mouth watering.

R.J. reached down and started stroking himself, moving his hand slowly from base to tip.

Lena licked her lips and felt herself lean forward. If she could just reach around Hal, just touch the tip of her tongue to that pearly drop at the tip. Hal's hands tightened on her hips and she felt herself lifted and turned.

"I said, straddle me. Neither R.J. nor I like disobedient subs. Do we?" Hal turned and saw R.J. standing a few steps away, slowly stroking himself. "See what you do to us, darling? You caused this."

"I did?" Lena couldn't move her eyes. She let Hal adjust her so that she was straddling him, the tips of her breasts brushing against his chest. She wondered if the light sprinkling of hair there was as soft as it looked and reached out a hand to touch it.

"Eyes on me, sub," Hal said, drawing her attention away from R.J. and focusing it back on him.

"Yes, Sir," she answered. Sub. He called her sub. Did that mean what she thought it did? In all the books she read that was how the Dom talked to the submissive. Were these men into BDSM? Her e-reader was filled with books on BDSM. The book R.J. had been reading from at her apartment was about BDSM. Did she even dare to ask them?

She felt a sharp smack on her bottom. "I don't think she's with us, R.J. I think she's in her head too much. We are going to need to work on that with her." Hal had noticed that Lena had a tendency to drift off and let her mind wander. They would need to fix that.

Slipping his hands under her thighs, he spread her legs wider and pulled her closer, pressing her breasts more firmly against his chest. "Lena, in the kind of relationship we want to have with you, you need to be present at all times. No side vacations. Just stay with us. If you can't do that, we will have to find ways to keep you engaged."

Wait, he said relationship, Lena thought. Maybe they wanted more than a one-night stand or a quick fling. Could she handle more? What the hell was she thinking? She hadn't met Melvin Ashcroft and had only known R.J. and Hal a few hours. There was no way she should even be thinking about a one-night stand, let alone a relationship. She usually didn't even think about dating a guy until she had known them a while and was definitely a third date rule girl.

Another smack to her ass. "Where did you go this time?" Hal asked, rubbing his hand over the place he had just slapped.

"I was just thinking that I had totally broken the third date rule." Lena giggled and laid her head on Hal's shoulder. It felt good to have someone hold her again. Now if he'd just stop slapping her ass and get on with the good stuff.

"Third date rule?" R.J. asked, watching as she leapt off to another thought. Her ass was going to be red before they even started to play, and she had too many clothes on.

"The third date rule means no touching until the third date," Lena explained, letting more of herself lean against Hal.

"No touching, you mean, no hand-holding and no good-night kiss. You don't let a guy touch you until the third date?" Hal asked. He had been on lots of dates and even more hookups. He wouldn't have even called back after the first date if the girl wouldn't at least let him kiss her. What kind of wimps had she been dating?

"You mean guys will go out with you for three dates before you let them touch you?" R.J. couldn't believe it either.

"Well, yeah. If they tried something on the first date I wouldn't go out with them again," Lena said, pulling back a little. What kind of girl did they think she was? Wait, she was sitting on the lap of a man she barely knew, half-naked. She was exactly that kind of girl right now.

"Baby, you need to give us guys more of a chance than that. You have to remember that around women like you most of our blood supply heads south and the caveman takes over. Hit them in the head with a club, throw them over our shoulder, and take them back to the cave and fuck them until they don't want anything else is the way most of us think, if we even think at all," Hal told her. He couldn't wait to tell Mel about this.

R.J. wanted to spank Hal now. Talk about side trips... Time to refocus on the task at hand, and did he have his hands full of it.

Hal tightened his hands around both of Lena's thighs and lifted her, pulling her even closer. There were just two thin pieces of material between him and heaven. "Put your arms around my neck, baby. Time to take this somewhere more comfortable," Hal said, standing and heading back to the bedroom.

Chapter Five

Lena wrapped her legs around Hal's hips and laid her head on his shoulder. He walked into the bedroom, kicking the door open, and carried her over to the bed. There he sat and slid his hands up her back, lifting her camisole as he did. "This needs to come off," he said, looking toward the door where R.J. was standing.

Lena turned her head away from Hal and saw R.J. leaning against the doorframe. "Aren't you going to join us?" she asked, her voice low and husky with need.

"I wasn't sure you wanted me. You both seem so cozy," he answered, not moving.

Hal rolled his eyes. He wasn't sure why R.J. had decided to be a drama queen all of a sudden, but he was going to let Lena handle it.

"It would be cozier if you were over here with us," Lena told him, smiling and reaching out one hand toward him.

R.J. was still naked and he came up behind Lena, kneeling on the floor. She let herself lean back, resting her back and shoulders against his chest. She turned her face to him. "Kiss me."

Hal still had his hands on her back under her top and when R.J. lifted his face from hers, he quickly pulled it off of her. "Beautiful," he said, turning her to face R.J. "Look at how pretty these breasts are," he said to R.J. as he reached around her and cupped each breast in his hand, lifting them for R.J. to see.

R.J. took the tip of each breast between his fingers. "Perfect, baby, I knew you would be. Do you like the feel of our hands on you? Master Hal holding you for me? Tell me, Lena, do you want more? I love to eat pussy. Has anyone ever eaten this pussy? I bet you taste like sweet nectar. Take a taste, Master Hal."

Hal slid one hand down her side and reached between her legs, spreading his to open hee and taking one finger, dipping it down between her folds. "I can smell her, R.J. she's ready for us." He moved that finger down, along the side of her clit, brushing the side, not touching it until he got to her juices. He swirled the finger around before bringing it up and putting it in his mouth.

Lena watched in fascination as his digit, glistening with her juices, moved past her face to his mouth.

Hal smacked his lips around his finger. "Umm, I can't wait to have the whole pie. I love pie," he said, smiling.

R.J. pinched her nipples tighter between his fingers and pulled them away from her body. The small bite of pain was enough to draw Lena's attention back to him. "You didn't answer me," he told her, a hint of disappointment in his voice.

"Oh, I...well, Simon wanted to try a sixty-nine once, but it didn't work so well, he said..." Did she want to tell these hot guys that the last man to eat her pussy said the rumors were true?

"What did he say, Lena?" R.J. asked, pinching her nipples a little harder.

"He said I tasted and smelled like rotten fish and I needed to keep myself cleaner. I shaved for him and everything, but he wouldn't touch me after that. I got fired a few days later and never heard from him again." Lena let her eyes fall to the floor, afraid to look at them.

"Lena," Hal said softly, "I can smell you from here and what I tasted was nothing like rotting fish. He was a fool." He turned her head toward him and took her lips in a soft kiss.

"My turn for a taste," R.J. said, spreading her legs wider. He brushed a soft kiss against her lips when Hal released her and then kissed his way down her torso, placing a soft kiss on each breast, just above the nipple. His eyes never left hers until he came to the apex of her thighs.

"Relax for us, baby, we won't do anything you won't like," Hal said, his hands reaching around to play with her breasts. He had felt her tense up when R.J. parted her folds.

R.J. lifted her thighs over his shoulders and, cupping her ass cheeks with his hands, used his thumbs to open her for his mouth.

He took a long lick from the top of her clit almost to her little brown hole. When Lena arched, trying to get his tongue back where she needed it, Hal pinched her nipples.

"Hold still, Lena. Let him take his taste. If you move too much he'll stop," Hal told her, tightening his grip on her.

R.J. lifted his head. "Give her something else to think about so I can give her what she needs," he told Hal.

With R.J. supporting her bottom, Hal maneuvered Lena so that she was sitting on the edge of the bed. When Hal was finished positioning them, he was kneeling beside her.

Lena turned her head and Hal was stroking his penis in a slow up-and-down motion. "This should keep you busy, while R.J. has his snack," he told her, brushing the tip of his cock over her lips and coating them with the small amount of pre-cum he had there.

Lena licked her lips, savoring the tart tangy taste he left there, eager for more. She leaned forward and reached one hand toward R.J., threading her fingers in his hair and pulling him closer.

"Hal, fix this," R.J. said, pulling away and shaking his head at her.

"What, what did I do now?" Lena whined as Hal quickly grasped both hands and put them behind her back.

"Leave them there or he will make me tie them," Hal told her as R.J. went back to what he had been doing. "He's very sensitive about this."

Lena wasn't sure she understood what Hal was talking about and was just about to ask when R.J. took her clit between his teeth, tugging gently. She landed back on her hands, arching her body. "Ohh," she moaned.

"Hal..." R.J. lifted his head long enough to say before going back to his task.

"Got it," Hal answered, turning her head toward him. "Open, honey. Let's keep that pretty little mouth busy for a while," he said, feeding his cock into her mouth when she opened it.

R.J. lifted his head and looked up. "That's a lovely sight," he said, watching as Hal slowly fed his engorged cock into Lena's waiting mouth.

"Hal, you will have to see and taste this. This is the prettiest pussy I've seen. Needs a little maintenance, but I will take care of that soon enough."

Lena briefly wondered what he meant by maintenance, but her attention was quickly drawn back to Hal as he fed more and more of his cock into her mouth. She was sure she couldn't take all of him, but he kept slowly advancing, going deeper and deeper. She wished she could use her hands, but she needed them for balance.

R.J. scooted her bottom closer to the edge of the bed, putting more of her weight on her hands. She fisted the comforter and held on for the ride.

R.J. licked from just above her anus to her clit. He seemed content to slowly lick her and did it several times before taking her clit between his lips again.

He tugged gently on her clit, gripping her bottom tightly with his hands. He lifted her, pulling her closer again and released her clit to lick again, this time stopping to curl his tongue and push it inside her. He began slowly pushing his tongue in and out of her.

Lena felt her body beginning to gather and knew she was close. Hal was holding her head with both hands and thrusting in and out of her mouth, his thrust matching the movements of R.J.'s tongue in her pussy.

R.J. lifted his head long enough to say, "She's close, brother. I'm going to finish her off."

Hal nodded and held her head tight between his hands, increasing the pace of his thrusts, fucking her mouth. Lena tried to relax her throat muscles but still gagged a couple times. Every time she did, Hal would stop and give her time to catch her breath, asking if she was okay before he went on.

R.J. and Hal seemed to be instinctively in sync with each other. When Hal intensified his thrusting in and out of her mouth, R.J. started nipping and pulling on her clit and thrusting one then two and finally three fingers inside of her. Just before Lena came, screaming their names, Hal released her head and pulled away.

Lena collapsed back on the bed, her legs dangling over R.J.'s shoulders, panting and trying to catch her breath.

Hal came shortly after Lena, his cum spurting over her chest. He collapsed on the bed, and R.J.'s head came to rest on her stomach, Hal's on her shoulder. Lena lay there panting for breath, waiting for the world to stop spinning around her.

Hal moved first, rolling to the side of the bed and pulling her with him, spooning her back to his front.

R.J. crawled up behind them, lying on his back beside Lena. Lena looked over and saw his erection standing there like a flagpole. "You didn't?" she asked.

"No, baby, climb on and take a ride, help a guy out," he said, a pleading look in his eyes.

Hal rolled over and grabbed a condom from the nightstand, handing it to her.

Lena took the package and looked at it then at R.J. "Open the package, take it out, and gently roll it down me," he told her, smiling and reaching down to grab the base of his cock to help her.

Lena got on her knees and leaned over, following his instructions until she had him covered.

"Now straddle me and have a seat, I'll help," he said, lifting her by the hips and pulling her until she straddled him. "Reach down and guide me until I'm at your core, then lower yourself slowly down," R.J. told her, guiding her by the hips.

Lena followed his directions, not sure she would accommodate his girth and length. "You're so..." she started breathlessly.

"We'll fit, darling, just relax and let me in," he told her, still holding her hips.

Hal had moved around behind her. "Not tonight, darling, but one night we will both take you at once. Has anyone ever played here?" he asked, spreading her cheeks and slowly rimming her asshole.

Lena tensed up and tightened her muscles, trying to keep him out. "No, Simon tried once but it hurt too bad." Lena had a little whimper in her voice when she answered him.

"Lena," R.J. pulled her attention back to him, "I know what that asshat did hurt, but does this?"

Lena let her body relax and focused on her feelings, not what she thought she should feel. "No, it really doesn't hurt, but I'm not sure I like it."

"Why don't you like it? If the three of us take you together, one of us will want to be there, honey. We will get you used to having something in there first, but it will happen. Mel is an ass man and yours is spectacular. He will want this little brown hole and often."

R.J. pulled her hips down and pushed his up, impaling her on him. He reached up and cupped her breasts. "Now use your legs and lift up and down, baby, ride me," he told her.

Lena felt something cool on her ass and tensed again. "Easy, it's just a little lube so I can play some," Hal told her, pressing his chest against her back and pushing his finger in a little deeper.

Hal held his finger still and let the movements of Lena's body move it in and out, letting her get used to the feeling of having something there. Later he would find a small plug for her to wear a few hours each day and gradually move her to bigger ones until she could take one of their cocks. They were not small men and it would take several days for her to get to the point where she could take one of them.

Lena liked the feeling of fullness. It wasn't as bad as she thought it would be. It was kind of erotic to have both men in her at once and she wondered how much different a cock would feel.

"I'm going to add another finger now, Lena. Are you doing okay?" Hal asked, leaning forward and placing a few light kisses against the back of her neck.

"Yeah, I'm good. It tingles and feels…" She let her voice trail off when R.J. released her breast and grabbed her hips again.

"Hold on, cowgirl, time to ride this out," he told her, pulling her forward until she braced her hands on his shoulders. Thrusting up with his hips, he pulled her down and increased the pace until she was bouncing up and down rapidly on him.

"Yes, that's it, honey, yes," R.J. called out, moving faster and faster until Lena fell on him with a scream as she had another orgasm.

"God, I…umm," she started, unable to finish her thought.

R.J. held her, thrusting, until he called her name and she felt the warmth of him coming inside her through the condom. "Wow, baby, that was awesome. Thank you," he said, gently brushing her sweat-dampened forehead with his lips.

"Yeah, it was, all of it." Lena sighed against his chest, snuggling down.

Hal slowly removed his fingers and went to start the shower. They were all damp with sweat and it was starting to cool off.

R.J. heard the shower start and relaxed a few minutes, letting Lena rest on his chest, her weight a comforting feeling on him.

He let his eyes close and heard Hal come back in the bedroom. "Up we go, sweetness. Let's go rinse off then we can all come back to bed," he told Lena, lifting her in his arms. He looked over his shoulder at R.J. "You just gonna lay there and bask in it or are you gonna come help me clean up our woman?" Not waiting for an answer, he carried Lena into the bathroom and sat her on the shower bench under the spray of warm water.

Lena let her head lean back against the shower wall and her eyes drift close. They would take care of her.

Hal heard R.J. rummaging in the cabinets and knew what he was looking for. He was surprised he had waited as long as he had.

R.J. came into the shower and saw how limp Lena was. "You gonna hold her, or should we put her on the bed?" he asked Hal.

"I'll hold her," Hal answered, picking Lena up and settling her in his lap.

"R.J.'s going to shave you now, honey. Just relax and let us take care of you."

"I shaved my legs last night. They won't be bad for a couple of days," Lena answered, confused.

"No, darling, I'm going to shave your pussy. I plan on spending a lot of time there and I don't like hair in my mouth," R.J. told her, moving her legs to the outside of Hal's so that when he spread his legs Lena's came open wider.

Lena's sex-addled brain told her it wasn't worth thinking about and she nodded and let her head loll back against Hal's shoulder. "Okay, whatever." She nodded, closing her eyes again and letting them take over.

Chapter Six

Lena woke the next morning to the sound of voices coming from the living room. She looked around and saw one of the men's shirts lying on the floor. She grabbed it and put it on, running her fingers through her hair. Expecting to see Hal and R.J., she was surprised when she saw another man with them.

"Come here, baby," Hal said, reaching for her and pulling her down on his lap.

"Good morning, sleepyhead," R.J. said, standing. He walked over to where she was sitting with Hal and placed a soft kiss on her lips before sitting on the arm of the chair and taking her hand.

She looked at the third man who was still sitting in the chair opposite where Lena was sitting with Hal. "Are you...?" she started to ask, but he spoke before she could finish.

Lena would know that voice from anyone's. He was the man she had interviewed with on the phone.

"Yes, Lena, I'm Melvin Ashcroft. I see you've become acquainted with my associates."

Lena wasn't sure if he was mad or just indifferent. "Yeah, umm. We met at your office yesterday," she answered, not sure how to handle the situation.

"Don't be a cold ass, Mel, you knew how this was going to turn out," Hal told his friend, tightening his hold on Lena when he felt her start to stiffen.

"Yes, well I can see once again I'm the odd man out. I'll be in my room if you decide you need me," Mel said, standing.

R.J. let go of Lena's hand and walked over to Mel, pushing on his shoulder to set him back in the seat. "Give it up, Mel. Just relax and get to know Lena. Don't be a jerk. None of this is her fault and you will not treat her like it is."

"Well, maybe if one of you had the sense to wait a day and not jump on the girl the minute you met her I wouldn't have to be an ass," Mel said, pushing R.J. back and crossing his arms over his chest.

Shit, Lena thought, are they going to fight? "Maybe I should leave. I can just get a taxi back to my car and go back to my apartment." She didn't want to be the cause of any trouble and struggled to get off of Hal's lap.

Hal tightened his hold. "You're staying here, Lena. We explained last night why it isn't safe for you to return to your apartment. That hasn't changed. Mel will be fine after he gets over his little tantrum. I will warn you he is going to want equal time."

Equal time? Lena wondered what that meant.

R.J. and Mel started yelling at each other and Hal stood up, taking Lena with him. "You don't need to hear this," he told her, walking back to the bedroom with her. "We will let them settle down a little. Why don't you get dressed and I'll take you down to one of the restaurants for breakfast? I think we both need some coffee."

"Okay. They won't hurt each other, will they?" Lena didn't want anyone to get hurt because of her.

Hal swiped his hand across his face. "They do this all the time. They just need to yell it out and all will be fine. I knew this was going to happen."

Lena cringed when she heard a crashing noise and started for the bedroom door. It sounded like they were doing more than yelling.

"No, honey, get dressed. They will be fine. It's how they have handled stuff since we first met in SEALs training," Hal said, cringing as they heard another crash.

Lena got dressed and wondered how they were going to get out of the apartment without going through the living room.

Once she was totally dressed, Hal grabbed her hand and said, "Follow me." He led her through the hall to his room and then through a door on the other side of the room. "This is the entrance to the stairs. We will walk one floor down and then catch the elevator to the third floor and the breakfast shop. It's also the fire escape if we can't get to the living room," he said as he opened the door and pulled her behind. Just before the door closed they heard another crash.

"Are you sure we shouldn't check on them?" Lena asked, biting her lip.

"Nope, come on, I'm hungry," Hal answered, pulling her down the stairs.

Lena and Hal were sitting in a booth in the back of the restaurant drinking coffee and talking when Mel walked up to the table.

"Skooch over, Lena," he said, sliding in the booth beside her.

Lena scooted over as close to the wall as she could get, trying to make herself as small as possible.

Hal reached across the table and took one of her hands from around the mug she was holding and threaded his fingers with hers. "It's okay. He's better now and he would never take anything out on you," he said reassuringly.

Lena wasn't so sure and kept her body tensed just in case, her mind searching for an escape plan. There weren't many options crammed against the side of the booth as she was but she figured she could always go under the table if they started throwing punches again.

"Where's R.J.? Do I need to call a cleaner and have the body disposed of?" Hal asked Mel, picking up his coffee to drink as if this was an everyday conversation.

"Bury a body? Wait, what, where's R.J.?" Lena was starting to panic. What were they talking about? Could Mel really have hurt R.J. that bad? She started pushing at Mel. She needed to get up and find R.J.

"Lena, chill," Hal said, seeing the panic on her face. "Mel, tell her."

"Tell me what? What did you do to him?" Lena was starting to get slightly hysterical and pushing at Mel and hitting him with her fists.

"Our little kitten can turn into a hellcat, can't she?" Mel said, grabbing both of her small fists in one of his massive hands and laughing.

Lena continued to struggle while Mel held both her hands in one of his. She tried to kick at him. "Where is he? What did you do with him? If you hurt him, I'll...I'll..." Lena couldn't think of a threat bad enough to convey what she would do but she would find something. "Let me go. I need to go see to him. Is he hurt? Where did you leave him?"

People at the other tables were starting to look around and a few were standing at all the noise Lena was making.

Hal watch with amusement while Lena continued to fight Mel, quite ineffectively. It was all he could do to keep himself from chuckling.

He knew that R.J. was fine and had probably stopped to do something before joining them for breakfast. Mel didn't look much the worse for wear and he was sure it had been one of their usual scuffles. The two men could and would fight about anything, something Lena would have to learn to deal with eventually.

"I can see why you needed to keep her mouth occupied. She has quite the vocabulary, doesn't she? We will have to work on that in the playroom very soon. I can't have her calling my mother those kinds of things when she comes to visit," Mel said with amusement in his voice as Lena continued to fight and cuss at him.

The waitress came over with the coffeepot, shook her head, and walked away. She was used to the owner's antics and knew when to mind her own business.

"Damn, I could have used a cup of coffee," Mel said, shaking his head. "If I let you free, will you stop cussing and fighting me?"

When Lena didn't slow down, he just shook his head and continued to hold her. "She has a lot of stamina, doesn't she? That's good. She's going to need it to keep up with all of us," Mel said to Hal, looking over Hal's shoulder and smiling as he saw R.J. walking toward them.

"Lena, stop and look up," he said, using his free hand to grab her head and turn it toward R.J., who slid into the booth beside Hal.

"I ran into Tucker. He told me that you two had a nice little handful back here. What set her off?" R.J. asked, motioning for the waitress.

"You're okay!" Lena exclaimed, now struggling to get free.

"Why wouldn't I be?" he asked, holding up four fingers when the waitress looked his way.

"Well, oh, shit, never mind. I'm just glad you two didn't kill each other," Lena said, sighing. Would she ever learn? She only had the one brother and he was several years younger so they had never fought growing up, but Trina had four brothers and they were always fighting about something.

"Let's order breakfast, I'm starving."

"R.J. just did. I'm going to let you go if you promise to stop hitting me," Mel said, relaxing his grip on her hands.

"I'm sorry about that. I should have waited for you to explain and realized that Hal was joking before I reacted," Lena said, looking at the table. This was her employer—or had been, up until she had lost her head and screwed his two associates. *Boy, did she know how to fuck up.* Great job, one minute, she was having mind-blowing sex and now she was unemployed again. She had known better. Now Mel was going to fire her for sure.

"It's okay, Lena, you didn't know I was joking," Hal said, reaching for her hand.

Lena quickly put both hands in her lap and continued looking at the table, wondering if she could get a job waiting tables.

R.J. looked at Hal. "What did you do now?"

"He asked if we needed to bury the body," Mel answered, slipping one arm across Lena's shoulders and pulling her closer to him.

All three men laughed and Mel squeezed her shoulder. "You'll get used to us soon enough, darling."

"I'm sorry. I'll get my things and be out of your home. If you would just let me out, I'll go call my cousin and see if she can come pick me up." Maybe staying with Jenna was her best option. Jenna's husband Kyle was one of the best bodyguards in the country. He would know how to protect her and she could always work at his club to pay him back.

"Lena, you're still not safe, and you have to start work on Monday," Mel said, moving her cup to the middle of the table.

The waitress came with refills for everyone. "I put in your order for four specials, Mel. Chuck will have them out soon. I told him they were for you guys," she said, filling the cups and walking off to deal with another table.

It took Lena a minute to process. When her brain realized what Mel had said, it took another minute for her body to react. She turned and threw her arms around him, planting a kiss on his lips. "Thank you, thank you. I didn't want to stay with her and I don't think I could work at a BDSM club. Thank you," she said quickly. She really hadn't wanted to work at Kyle's BDSM club, Club de Fleurs.

Mel looked questioningly at Hal, wondering what path Lena's mind was taking now.

"Her mental road trips are something we need to address, but I think she's thanking you for letting her keep her job," Hal said, watching Lena plant little kisses all over Mel.

"Is she like this all the time?" Mel asked, referring to the way she flitted back and forth.

"Yeah, from what we can tell I think she has a little trouble focusing, but I know how to work on that," R.J. said, an evil grin on his face.

"I'm sure you do," Mel said, laughing. R.J. was the strictest of the three Doms and he would be the one who would do most of Lena's training and discipline. Mel saw a lot of punishments in her future.

Lena was just about to ask what they were talking about when the waitress brought their food. The table grew silent as they all ate their platters of eggs, bacon, and biscuits and gravy. Their coffee was refilled again and R.J. finished what Lena couldn't, stating he was "just a growing boy."

Breakfast finished, the men went to the condo, where they all sat talking and getting to know one another better. Mel seemed to have gotten over the mood he was in and he kept Lena close by. All three men were touching her often and they didn't let her out of their sight. One of them even followed her to the bathroom when she needed to go. "I think I'm safe here, guys, I don't need a shadow," she told them when it got to be a little much.

That turned into a discussion of her safety and what she needed to do. By the time they were done, she was crying and wished she had never ever met Simon or Frank, the jerks.

"Do you really think I'm in danger?" she asked more than once, not really wanting to believe it. She couldn't believe she had been so naïve.

She got so worked up that Mel finally insisted on taking her into the bedroom and laying her down for a nap. She protested but after he teased and played with her and a couple mind-blowing orgasms, she finally settled down and slept.

Mel went back to talk logistics with Hal and R.J., and they decided that Lance Lewis and his brothers Luke and Leif would be assigned to watch Trina, and that Tucker Hague and his team would be sent to watch over Lena's family. They also decided to move all the furniture from her apartment to the basement of their building and pay off her lease. None of them wanted her going back there again.

Everything decided, the men sat back to relax and Mel went to sneak a peek at Lena and make sure she was still resting. They knew when she found out what they had done she would be pissed, but it couldn't be helped.

When Mel returned to the room the men had taken a vote and decided he could be the one to tell Lena about what they had done. "If she gives you any trouble I'll take her to the playroom," R.J. told him. In his opinion, she had been topping from the bottom entirely too much.

"Does she even know about the playroom?" Mel asked.

"No, we decided that the three of us should show it to her," Hal answered, hoping to fend off a fight before it could start.

"Well, at least you waited for me to do something." Mel was still pissed that they had played with Lena before he could arrive home and join them.

"Mel, like I tried to explain this morning, I had every intention of waiting, but the girl wanted it bad. You should have seen the outfit she put on to play poker in and the moves she was making."

"So, big bad Dom that you are, you couldn't resist one little sub topping from the bottom." Mel had his arms crossed over his chest. He still wanted to punch someone.

"Look, if it makes you feel better, Hal and I will disappear tonight and you can have her all to yourself." R.J. really didn't want to leave but he knew how he would feel if things had been reversed and Hal and Mel had met Lena first and played with her when he was not available.

"No, we're good, letting me beat the shit out of you this morning helped," Mel said, laughing and clapping R.J. on the back.

They heard a noise and turned toward the bedrooms, where Lena was coming down the hall, her feet bare, her hair sleep tousled. She was wearing another camisole top, in a peach color. This one was form-fitting but also left a few inches of stomach bare to their eyes. Today she wore it with a pair of yoga pants.

Mel walked up to her and pulled her into his arms. "Did you sleep well, honey?" he asked, brushing a soft kiss over her lips.

Lena wasn't as comfortable with him as she was with R.J. and Hal. A situation he planned on fixing during the evening, even if it took him all night.

Lena looked into his eyes shyly and nodded her head, stepping away from him and walking over to sit on the end of the couch, far away from all the men.

"What's the matter, honey?" Hal asked, getting up from the chair where he had been and plopping down beside her.

"I'm still not sure this is a good idea," Lena said, twirling one finger in her hair.

Hal put his arm around her and pulled her closer. "Why not, Lena?"

"I'm not sure. I mean...I don't know any of you very well and well, are you sure I'm in danger? Nobody ever told me who was paying all of you." She pushed away from Hal and started pacing the room.

"Lena, don't worry about who's paying. Sit down. I didn't want to show you these things, but I think you need to see them," Mel said, leading her to the dining room table. He grabbed his briefcase and a laptop computer and pulled a chair next to hers.

He didn't want to tell her that he had taken the case as a favor to his friend at the FBI. He was afraid that if she knew the FBI was paying she would think they were trying to prove her guilty.

"This is video surveillance the FBI took of your apartment," he said, opening a file on the computer and starting a video. It showed her apartment. Apparently, it had been taken when she wasn't home. There were several men in her apartment and they were going through her things. She watched as one of them planted little devices all over the room and another one was positioning what looked like small cameras around.

"These men have been identified as working for some of the men you approved loans for. What they are doing is planting listening devices and cameras around your apartment," Mel explained.

He pulled up another video of her inside her car. She was dressed as she did for her job interviews and it was apparent she was on the way to one. "They have been following you since before you were let go at the bank. They think you are the one who reported the scam to the Feds and are after you to keep you quiet."

"But I never did anything. I didn't even know what was going on," Lena protested.

"Lena, you may know more than you think you know. Later today I will sit with you and ask you a series of questions that will help us figure that out. Right now you need to get dressed. We are going down for lunch," Mel told her firmly. After seeing what was in her kitchen they knew she hadn't been eating well and planned on taking care of that.

"I don't think I'm hungry," Lena said, not moving.

Mel looked at R.J. Time to let her know how this was going to work.

"Lena, Mel didn't ask if you were hungry. He told you to go get changed," R.J. told her, using his Dom voice. A voice most subs knew not to disobey.

"I don't want to go for lunch, you guys go. I'll just stay here. I think I'm going to take a shower," Lena said, standing and turning to go to her bedroom. So much had happened in the last twenty-four hours that she was having trouble processing it all.

She needed to call Jenna and let her know what was going on. Jenna would know what to do. Her husband was in the security business. They could call him.

She should probably call her parents and her brother to let them know also. They were going to be mad at her for putting them in the middle again, snd wouldn't believe she hadn't done something.

She didn't realize that all three men were following her until she sat on the bed and reached for her purse. She saw them standing just inside the door. "What? I said I'm going to take a shower and I have some calls to make first."

"Lena, do you want to explore a relationship with the three of us?" Hal asked. The three men were standing side by side with their arms crossed over their chests and legs spread shoulder width apart. "I thought you did by your actions last night, but if you don't, that's fine. You can stay here as our guest and employee and we will do our best to protect you. If you want more than that you need to understand there will be some rules you need to follow. What do you want to do?" He cocked one eyebrow and they all waited for her answer.

Lena thought a minute. Did she want to explore more with these men? Could she handle a relationship with three men? Would she be enough woman for all of them? "What kind of relationship exactly are we talking about?" she asked. She thought she knew, but she wanted them to spell it out and make sure they were all on the same page. She had jumped in with both feet before and look where it had gotten her. She didn't want to make the same mistake three times in a row.

Hal walked over and sat beside her on the bed. "Lena, Mel, R.J., and I are all Dominants. Do you know what that means?"

"That you like to give orders and have them followed," she answered. She wasn't sure that was exactly right and was sure they would correct her.

"Not exactly," R.J. answered, coming over to sit on her other side. He took one of her hands and held it. "It means that we need your submission. What do you think submission means?"

"Doing everything you tell me to," she answered.

"Submission to us means giving your trust and your body to us. You freely give all of yourself to us and trust us to take care of you. Some D/s relationships are twenty-four hours seven days a week. That is not what we want. We will expect you to obey us, and when we make a request of you for you to either do it or have a logical argument why you shouldn't. If you tell us in a respectful tone why you don't want to do something we have asked you to, we will listen and consider your reasons. That doesn't mean we will give in to you. We may have reasons for asking you to do something that you don't understand. Most of the requests we make outside the bedroom or playroom, or when we are not in a scene, will be for your health or safety or both. When Mel told you to get dressed for lunch, it was for your health. We saw what you have for food in your home and not only was it insufficient to feed a toddler, it was not healthy. We want you strong and healthy for us. We want you to be able to keep up with all of us. Your face is sallow and you have deep dark circles under your eyes. When was the last time you had a good night's sleep?"

Lena quickly answered, "Last night."

"Honey, that's not what I call a good night's sleep. I know either Hal or I was waking you up several times during the night and you were up early with us this morning," R.J. said, a twinkle in his eyes. "Tell the truth—when did you last get at least seven hours of sleep in one night?"

"I've been trying to find a job and my apartment building can get noisy and...you're right. I haven't been eating or sleeping well," she finally gave in and answered.

Mel knelt in front of her and laid one hand on her knee. "Darling, all we want is to take care of you. You need to start eating more. You need to get more rest. Let us take care of you."

Lena couldn't help it, she started crying. She was tired and knew she hadn't been eating right. How long had it been since someone had wanted to take care of her? Both Frank and Simon had just gone out with her because of what she could do for them. After her father had found out that she didn't want to stay and help on the farm, he had written her off and forbade her mother to contact her. Even her baby brother didn't want anything to do with her.

"What kind of rules are we talking about and how long would this 'relationship' last?" Lena asked. Maybe she could try this and see what happened. It would be nice to be wanted for herself and not for what she could do for someone for a change.

"The rules are simple. You address us with respect at all times. If there is something you don't agree with or don't want to do when we are not playing, you need to respectfully ask why we want you to do whatever and tell us why you don't want to do it," Hal started explaining what they wanted from her.

"When we are in a scene or in the bedroom or playroom the word 'red' stops everything. When you use that word we will stop whatever we are doing and talk about why you needed to stop. After we talk and work things out we will either stop for the time being or continue," R.J. went on to tell her.

"When you are bratty or disrespectful or disobey or flat-out refuse to do something you will be punished. Topping from the bottom like you were last night will also result in punishment," Hal explained.

"Wait a minute. I didn't do anything last night, and what do you mean by punishment?"

"Lena, last night you wanted something from us. I had told you that we were going to give you the evening to get to know us before you had to make a decision about staying and playing with you. You wanted more than that and with your actions and words, you manipulated us into playing with you. Didn't you?" R.J. said, taking her chin between his fingers and turning her face so that she was staring into his ice-blue eyes.

Lena nodded and couldn't help the grin that came to her face, remembering what she had done and what the results had been.

"You know we are going to have to punish you for that and for what happened when Mel told you to change, don't you?" R.J. asked, still holding her chin.

"What do you mean by punish?" Lena asked again. They hadn't answered that part of her question.

"Punishments will differ for different things. It will depend on what you have done, on how you will be disciplined. R.J. and I will decide on your correction for last night. Mel will decide how he wants to deal with you for disobeying him," Hal said, turning her face toward him when R.J. released her.

"Lena, just remember that 'red' will always work whether we are in a punishment or playing. 'Red' will always stop what is happening so that we can talk about it. We will push your limits, but it will never be more than you can take and we will never hurt you," Mel told her, tightening his grip on her knee. "Now I'm going to pick out some clothes for you to change into so we can all go down and have lunch. Then we will bring you back up here and you will take a nap. This evening we will all go to our playroom where Hal and R.J. will take corrective measures for your actions of last evening."

"I can pick out my own clothes." Lena didn't understand why Mel needed to pick out her clothes.

Chapter Seven

*T*his is going to be a challenge and it will take all of us to tame her, Mel thought to himself, catching the look in Hal and R.J.'s eyes. They were all in agreement. The three of them had been friends and worked together so long that they could communicate with looks and facial gestures.

"Lena, as part of your punishment, I will pick out your clothes and you will wear what I give you and only what I give you. I will also select what you will have for lunch. Do you have any food allergies or intense dislikes I need to know about?" When she shook her head no, Mel continued on. "If you do not wear what I give you or if you add or remove anything from what you are given, you will feel the consequences. If you do not eat the food I give you, you will be punished. Understand?"

When Lena nodded, Mel walked over to the closet where they had put her clothes after carefully checking each item for electronic listening devices and picked out a button-down blouse and short skirt with a pair of flats for her to wear.

"Put these on and be in the living room in ten minutes. It will be five swats for the first minute you are late and one for every minute after that," Mel told her, handing her what he had chosen and walking out of the room.

Lena looked quickly at what was in her hand. Not too bad of a choice, something she might have chosen for herself. There was no underwear, so she assumed she should just wear what she had on.

She ran into the bathroom to wash up and quickly change, adding a little blush and lip gloss. They were right. She did have dark circles under her eyes and her complexion was sallower. She looked old and washed out. She did need to eat better and rest more.

Wondering if she still had any time left, she slipped on her shoes and walked out to where the men were waiting.

"Very nice, baby, come here," Mel said, crooking his finger and motioning her toward him. They were going to have to take her shopping soon. She had very few outfits and nothing that looked like it would work for the club. He couldn't wait to take her to his friend Kyle's club.

Lena walked over to where Mel was sitting and stood in front of him. He motioned for her to turn in a circle. She twirled then stopped, facing him.

"What do you have on under your skirt?" Mel asked, a stern look on his face.

"Panties, silly," Lena said, laughing.

"Where did you get the panties, Lena?" Hal asked as he watched Mel's eyes bug out.

"I'll handle this, Harold," Mel said.

Lena knew she was in trouble and tried to figure out a way to get out of it.

"Lena, answer the question," Mel said, his voice getting darker and deeper.

"I was wearing them already," she answered, looking down at the floor.

"I believe I told you to wear what I gave you and only what I gave you."

"Yes, Sir. I didn't know I was supposed to take off what I already had on." She tried to make an excuse for herself but could see he wasn't buying it.

"Did you take off your other shirt and pants without my telling you?" Mel asked. It was all he could do to keep the amusement out of his voice, he was having so much fun.

Oh, I'm so not getting out of this easy, Lena thought, wondering what she should do to make it easier on herself. "No, sir," she answered, not knowing what else to do.

"Did you think I meant for you to wear panties, Lena?"

Oh shit. If she answered yes, she was in trouble. She had known when she saw what he handed her what he meant. If she answered no, she was in trouble, too, because then he would ask if she had defied him on purpose. Then she would be in trouble for that topping from the bottom thing again. Ugh, so what did she do?

Hanging her head, she stared at the floor and mumbled, "I'm sorry, sir."

"What was that? I didn't hear you."

"I'm sorry?" she asked.

"Are you asking me if you're sorry, Lena?" Mel was really starting to have fun now.

Now she was starting to get mad. "No, I'm not sorry. I put the damned panties on. What are you going to do about it?" she yelled, losing her temper.

"Oh no, you are in for it now, darling," R.J. said behind her.

She had forgotten they were there and without thinking whipped around and told him with a stern voice, "You stay out of this."

"Well, boys, I see our kitten can be a little bit of a tiger. I was going to wait until this evening to do this but I think you need the attention now. R.J., would you care to join us?" Mel asked as he stood and reached for Lena's hand.

Lena took his outstretched hand with trembling fingers and looked to Hal for help.

"I can't help you now," Hal said, chuckling.

"Hal, if you wouldn't mind calling and ordering some lunch from the diner before you join us in the playroom," Mel said, walking down the hall, pulling Lena behind him.

Lena followed along behind Mel, wondering what she had gotten herself into now. She was a little excited and a little scared. Even though she hadn't known the men very long she knew she could trust them.

Mel entered the code to unlock the playroom door and led Lena inside. Lena had never seen a playroom before and was a little amazed to see some of the things she had only read about. She had looked up a few things on the internet, but it wasn't like seeing them in real life.

She walked over to what she assumed was a spanking bench and ran her hand across the padded leather seat, wondering if they were going to use it or what they had planned. She roamed around the room, looking at things, sometimes reaching her hand out to touch something only to pull it back as if she were burnt.

When she reached the wall where all the canes, whips, and paddles were, she glanced at what was there quickly before reaching out and picking up one cane. She slapped the palm of her hand with it before wincing and putting it back.

Mel and R.J. let her roam around, acquainting herself with what was in the room.

Hal joined them and all three men stood watching Lena. While Lena was looking around, the men quickly took off their shirts and kicked their shoes to one side.

When Lena turned around, her knees grew weak and her mouth started to water. Even though she had seen R.J. and Hal the night before, she still couldn't believe how handsome they were. Mel was everything she had dreamed of when she had heard his voice on the phone. She had no idea how she was going to get any work done with these three around.

"Lena," Hal called, crooking his finger for her to come to where they were standing.

"Yes," she answered, walking over to them.

"Today we let you explore and touch things. This is the only time you will be allowed to do that. You never enter this room without one of us. If we find you in here without permission, you won't sit comfortably for a week or more," R.J. said, walking around her and standing behind her.

He slipped his arms around her and reached for the buttons of her shirt, methodically unfastening each one until her shirt hung open.

"Was the bra something you already had on and just decided to keep on?" Mel asked, his eyes blazing with heat.

"Um...yeah. I really didn't know you wanted me to go without underwear." Lena thought it might be worth one more shot at getting herself out of this mess.

"After our little session this afternoon, I don't think you'll be making that mistake again," Mel said, stepping forward and flicking open the front fastening of her bra, freeing her breasts to his and the others' eyes.

R.J. slipped her top and bra off her shoulders and threw them to the pile where the men had placed their shirts. "Kick your shoes off, darling," he told her, sliding his hands down her arms.

Lena shivered and kicked her shoes over to the wall behind Mel and Hal. "Now, slip off the skirt, leave the panties for now," R.J. said, stepping back to give her room to remove her skirt.

Lena complied and stood there, resisting the urge to cross her arm over her bare breasts, and waited for the next instruction.

"Come with me." Mel led her over to the huge bed they had placed in the center of the back wall of the room and sat on the side of her. "Stand right here."

She stood between his spread legs and waited to see what he would do next. "Hands at your side. Don't move, no matter what I do. How well you can obey will determine what I do next. What's your safe word?"

"Red, sir," she answered, her voice soft and breathless. Her panties were starting to get damp and they hadn't even touched her yet.

"Use it if you need to, but if you use it and one of us thinks you shouldn't have, everything stops. Understand?" Mel told her.

Lena nodded and stood waiting. Mel put one finger in his mouth, wetting it before reaching out and touching it lightly to one nipple. He blew a puff of warm air on her wet skin and watched as the little bud grew larger. He repeated the action with the other nipple, not touching her anywhere else.

Lena stood as still as she could, anticipation building as she wondered what else he was going to do.

Mel looked at R.J. and some form of silent communication happened between the two men. R.J. nodded and walked over to a large cabinet on the wall. His back was to Lena and she couldn't see what he was doing for sure, but she thought he took something out of one of the drawers before walking back over to them.

Lena heard the sound of a doorbell and Hal said, "That's lunch. I'll bring it in here."

Hal came back with a large bag and four drinks. Lena started to walk over and help him when Mel grabbed her hips with both hands and held her in place. "I told you not to move." He looked at R.J. again and R.J. went to help Hal.

R.J. pulled a table over and Hal set the food out on it. There were several containers and Lena couldn't tell what they had, but it smelled wonderful. She didn't realize how hungry she had been getting.

Hal put a straw in one of the cups and brought it over to Mel. Mel held it up to her lips. "Drink."

Lena took a long drink, enjoying the taste of milk, something she hadn't been able to afford for a while. "Good girl."

Lena stood, eyes focused on Mel, and didn't see what R.J. and Hal were doing until Hal brought over a plate loaded with fried chicken, mashed potatoes, and coleslaw.

Mel tore a piece of meat off the chicken and held it to Lena's lips. She opened and took the bite, savoring the taste. Mel set the plate on the bed beside him and took one of Lena's hands in his.

He pulled her onto his lap and proceeded to feed her everything on the plate bite by bite until it was gone. R.J. brought over another plate and gave it to Mel, which he ate between feeding Lena bites.

When everything was gone, Hal gathered up the dirty dishes and took them out of the room. When he returned Mel was telling Lena how well she had done and was passionately kissing her.

"Lena, you did very well during lunch, but now we have a punishment to administer. If you do well, there will be a reward at the end," Mel told her, running his hands up and down her back.

Lena was still a little starstruck from the kiss and just nodded her head. Mel helped her stand between his legs again and slid his hands up her body to cup her breasts. "These are beautiful, but I think they could use a little something. R.J., what did you find for our girl?"

R.J. held his hand out beside Lena where she couldn't see what he had. When Lena turned her head to see what he had, Mel reached out and grabbed her chin with one hand. "Eyes on me, sweetheart."

Hal took the items R.J. had chosen for Lena and stood off to the side where she couldn't see them. R.J. moved behind Lena and reached around her with both arms and cupped her breasts, lifting them for Mel.

Mel leaned forward and took each of her nipples between his fingers, pinching and pulling them, rolling them between his fingers. After doing this for a few minutes, he leaned forward and took her right nipple in his mouth, sucking on it and gently pulling it between his teeth, biting it softly.

He reached to Hal and out of the corner of her eye Lena saw Hal put something in Mel's hand but couldn't tell what it was. Mel held his hand out palm up and showed her the object Hal had given him. Lena looked at it, thinking it was an earring at first. She started to ask when it dawned on her. "No, I don't think so," she said, covering both breasts with her hands.

She heard R.J. growl behind her and cringed a little, realizing what she had just done. Mel's eyes turned cold and she could see his expression change from one of enjoyment and desire to what she hoped was disappointment and not anger. His smoke-colored eyes turned dark, almost black, and he reached up and took her hands, moving them to her side. "I will remind you this one time only, keep your hands at your side. That will increase your count. R.J., do you have anything to add?"

Lena could feel her heart rate increase as the tension in the room increased. A tear slid down her face and it was all she could do to stand there. Her flight instinct was kicking in and she wanted to run and hide.

She couldn't believe how stupid she had been. She knew better. Even though she was new to all of this, she had read enough books that she knew what was expected of her. Compared to some of the books she had read they were being very lenient with her. Most of the Doms in her books would have had her ass blistered by now.

They were being so nice to her and how was she treating them? By disrespecting them and disobeying. They had given her a job, which she hadn't even started yet. They had promised to protect her from the men who were after her and they were letting her stay in their home. Why was she such a screwup? She deserved it if they put her out on the streets and fired her.

"Lena?" Hal said her name softly, bringing her back from her thoughts.

"Yes," she answered, trying to stop the tears that had begun running down her face.

Mel pulled her into his lap and R.J. appeared with a warm cloth to wipe her face. "What were you thinking, honey? The truth," he asked softly, holding her tight.

She sniffled and answered, "I was thinking about what a screwup I am and how you've been nice to me and how I don't deserve it and how I should leave and find another place to stay, because now I don't have a job and you're going to throw me out for messing up and that my parents and brother are right, I can't do anything without making a mess of it and..." She stopped and started sobbing again.

Mel pulled her tighter against his chest when she buried her face in his shoulder.

R.J. and Hal sent Mel a series of signals and stepped out of the room to talk.

Chapter Eight

"Crap, how the hell have people been treating her? I knew she was submissive, but this poor girl has been through hell to think so badly of herself," R.J. said, hitting the wall with his fist.

"I know. Shit, she has no self-esteem whatsoever. We are going to have to be very careful with her. I knew it was bad, but I didn't think it was this bad," Hal said, hands fisted by his side.

"That background report we got was not near thorough enough. I'll have somebody's ass before this is all done. We need to start by finding out what kind of shit her parents put her through and then when we get enough evidence to put away those assholes who did this to her, I get to spend ten minutes alone with each of them. They will think twice before trying this shit again, I'll tell you."

"I know, before you mash them to a pulp I think Mel and I will each take a turn," Hal told him, turning to go back in the playroom before Lena noticed they were gone and thought they had deserted her. It sounded like she had been let down a lot in her life.

When they got back in the room, Lena had stopped crying and Mel was talking softly to her. They couldn't hear what he was saying until they got closer. "Yes, baby, we still want you. We won't send you away. Yes, you are still getting a correction. You still deserve a punishment. Just because you had a meltdown doesn't mean we don't care for you anymore. You still have a job to start Monday. We still want you and we are still going to protect you. Right, Hal and R.J?" Mel asked, as if they had been there all along and heard everything he said.

They both moved to her. R.J. knelt at her side in front of Mel and Hal got down on one knee in front of her, to Mel's side.

Hal gently took her face in his hands and brushed a soft kiss over her lips. "Pretty little subs who have bad days will still get what they need, baby. Just because things got a little messed up doesn't mean we won't take care of you. We wouldn't make you leave," he said, releasing her face and turning her toward R.J.

"Honey, we still want you. If you don't believe me, here's the proof," he told her, taking her hand and pulling it down to cover his steel-hard cock.

Lena tightened her fingers over him and giggled. "I bet you do. Is it painful?"

"Sugar, I think you're going to be in as much pain as we all are before this is over," R.J. promised.

R.J. and Hal stood up and took a step to the side, allowing Mel to stand with Lena in front of him.

Hal stepped away and returned with a warm wet cloth and handed it to Lena. "Clean up your face, darling. No more crying unless it's in sexual frustration or because your ass hurts. Understand?"

Lena felt a pulse go through her body and nodded as she went from feeling sorry for herself to arousal.

Mel picked up the nipple clamp from the bed and showed it to her again. "Hold out your hand, Lena."

Lena held out her hand and Mel took her little finger, fitting the clamp over it and tightening. "It will feel worse on your nipple, but this first time I will tighten them slowly and watch your face while I am doing it. If it gets to be too much you can use your safe word, red," he told her, reminding her that she could always call a stop to things.

Lena nodded and waited for them to proceed. "Boys, get her ready for me," Mel said to R.J. and Hal.

The men moved Lena back a few steps and each of them took one of her nipples between their fingers, pinching and pulling them before taking them with their lips and sucking on them.

Lena had to admit to herself that she liked this part even if the clamps themselves scared her. She felt her panties getting wet and knew it was going to be okay.

Mel had made such a big fuss over her panties she wondered why he had let her leave them on. She wanted to ask him and although he hadn't specifically told her to be quiet she had a feeling that asking a question would be frowned upon.

"You aren't doing a good enough job of distracting her, guys, she just drifted off again. Lena," Mel said sharply, snapping his fingers in front of her face, "you need to stay here with us, baby. Eyes on me."

Lena looked up and smiled. "I did it again, I'm sorry," Lena answered. She really was going to have to learn to do something about her focus. Maybe meditation or yoga. Yoga was supposed to be good for that type of thing. Maybe she could find some books on it on the internet and download them to her e-reader. She needed to try to remember to do that and maybe she could do an internet search on how to focus her thoughts. Maybe some brain games or something like that.

"Ouch, what was that?" She let out a little scream and jumped when she felt a sharp pain in her right nipple. She looked down and saw that Mel was pinching her nipple hard.

"That's one way to get her focus back on us," he told R.J. and Hal with a grin on his face, turning back to look in Lena's eyes. Her eyes were watering and she was giving him a dirty look.

"That wasn't nice," she said, sticking her bottom lip out and her voice petulant.

"I'm going to put the clamp on now, Lena, and I don't want you drifting off to wherever it is you go in your mind while I do it. Pay attention and eyes on me so I can tell if it's hurting you too much," Mel told her, cupping her breast with one hand and applying the clamp with the other.

Lena felt a slight pressure at first and as he turned the screw it became tighter and tighter. She pulled her top lip between her teeth and bit it, trying to resist the urge to reach up and pull the thing off her nipple. Hal leaned over and whispered in her ear, "Just relax and breathe, give it a minute."

Lena tried to relax and soon the feeling was morphing into want and need. She could feel the wetness between her legs and was glad they had let her keep her panties on.

Mel put the other clamp on then turned her for Hal and R.J. to see. "What do you think, boys?" he asked them, cupping her breasts from behind and lifting them for Hal and R.J to admire.

Hal and R.J. both told her how beautiful she looked and praised her for taking the clamps so well before Mel turned her back around. "Now I believe you are due a spanking for wearing these without permission. I know I didn't specifically tell you not to wear them, but I did say to wear only what I gave you. From now on you will know," Mel told her when he could see she was starting to protest.

Lena was anxious and excited. She wondered if it would be anything like what happened in her books. The times she had tried it with Simon and Frank it hadn't worked out very well. She knew this would be different.

"Let's get started before she drifts off again," Mel said to Hal and R.J.

He reached out and ripped her panties off her. "Hey! Those were one of my nicer pairs. Trina gave those to me and she doesn't buy cheap stuff," Lena said with a huff.

"Baby, I'll buy you all kinds he can rip off of you, when he allows you to wear them," Hal whispered in her ear, licking the lobe before taking it between his teeth and pulling.

"Enough, come here, honey," R.J. said, taking her from Hal and pulling her up against him. He took her lips in a kiss that had her raising up on her toes and panting when he was done.

He turned her to Mel. "Drape yourself over that lap," he told her, guiding her face down over Mel's lap.

"Since this is your first time it will be a count of twenty-five. Ten from me for wearing the underwear. Ten from R.J. for snapping at him and five from Hal because he whines if he's left out and nobody should have to see that."

"He's right, it's not pretty," R.J. commented with a chuckle.

Hal walked around behind her. "I'm going first, honey. I'm going to start slow and warm you up for R.J. and Mel."

Mel adjusted her position on his lap so her ass was in the air and her toes barely touched the ground. She couldn't quite reach the floor with her hands so she wrapped them around Mel's calf for balance.

She felt Mel place one hand in the notch between her hip and her waist, steadying her, and she didn't feel like she was going to fall anymore.

R.J. knelt in front of her, moving her hair out of her face so that she could look at him. "Eyes on me, honey." From this position, he could observe her reactions and let Hal and Mel know if things were getting to be too much for her. Until they got to know her better one of them would always watch her during punishments and play to make sure they weren't pushing her too far.

Hal started by rubbing his hands over her lower back, buttocks, and upper thighs. Then he squeezed her buttocks, sensitizing them and making her more aware of the feelings back there. The rubbing and the squeezing felt good, almost like a massage. Just when Lena was starting to think that this was going to be okay, she heard a slap and felt a heavy thud right on the center of her bottom that was followed by a sharp slap to each ass cheek, which really stung. She looked up at R.J. and he had a smirk on his face. "Wait for my turn," he said, grinning.

Hal gave her another sharp smack on each cheek and ran his hands around and over the skin, holding the heat from the slaps in.

"All warmed up, Mel," he said, trading places with R.J.

He lifted her head and kissed her gently, licking at the few tears she had started to shed. "That part wasn't so bad, but this next part will be worse. Mel and R.J. aren't as easygoing as I am," Hal warned her.

Mel took his turn next, starting the same way Hal did before placing ten sharp smacks on her bottom, the blows coming quickly and randomly so that Lena couldn't brace herself and prepare for the them.

Mel was finished quickly and the tears were flowing freely when he was done. He sat her up on his lap and told her, "Time for a little break before R.J. takes his turn." He held her and rocked her, helping her dry her face and giving her a bottle of water to drink.

After about five minutes, R.J. stood in front of them, a paddle in his hand. "Hold your hand out, Lena." She did and he smacked the palm of her hand with the paddle. "The smacks I give you won't be much harder than that. Next time you snap at me I will use a crop so think hard before you speak," he said, helping her arrange herself over Mel's lap again and walking around behind her.

He started the same way Mel and Hal had by squeezing and rubbing her bottom, but she felt it more now. Her bottom was more sensitive and she knew that the paddle was going to feel worse on her bottom than it had on her hand.

Hal knelt down in front of her, and instead of her holding to Mel's leg, she laid her head on his shoulder, with his arms around her upper torso supporting her.

The first strike of the paddle felt like fire and Lena jumped and let out a little scream. R.J. didn't drag it out and finished his part of the punishment quickly.

Hal disappeared and R.J. took her from Mel, holding and soothing her before picking her up and carrying her out of the room. She put her arms around him and nuzzled her face into his neck. He carried her into the bathroom that was attached to the bedroom they had given her, placing her in Hal's arms. Hal was already sitting in the tub full of warm water and he pulled her down to sit between his legs. R.J.

and Mel quickly stripped and joined them. The water level was high, reaching just under Lena's breasts as she sat in Hal's lap and they floated on the water.

She reached for one of the clamps to remove it and Hal grabbed her hand. "Not yet, honey, let R.J. and Mel do it."

Lena relaxed back against him, waiting to see what would happen next. R.J. and Mel each cupped a breast with one hand and then started loosening the clamps with the other. As the pressure was released Lena let a sigh of relief escape her and she relaxed. As the blood began to return to her squished nipples she felt the burn and started wiggling. "Oh, oh, oh," she panted, reaching for them.

Before she could, R.J. and Mel each took one in their mouth and began sucking, providing the relief she needed. They continued for several minutes before releasing her with a pop and settling back in the tub.

"My turn now, baby. I want a little taste of what Hal had last night," Mel said, fisting his rigid cock and stroking it.

Lena nodded and leaned forward to take him in her mouth. Mel rose on his knees to meet her and she wrapped her lips around his shaft, taking the head in her mouth and tasting the drop of pre-cum there. She pulled back and released him, swirling her tongue around the head like she would a tasty ice cream cone. Fisting one hand around the base of his cock, she relaxed her jaw and opened her mouth as wide as she could, taking the head and part of the shaft into her mouth. She was determined to make him fit and released him before taking a deep breath and trying again. On the second try, she got more of Mel's monster cock into her mouth and took about him partially down her throat.

She had moved her legs on the outside of Hal's and was on her knees, bent over, legs spread, leaving her bottom almost in Hal's face.

Hal couldn't resist the sight in front of him and reached with both hands to spread her cheeks, baring her little rosette. Taking the tip of his tongue, he touched her there, feeling her jerk. "Don't bite Mel, Lena, you won't like what happens if you do," he told her, licking around her hole and stabbing his tongue inside it.

He held her open with his thumbs while his hands reached around and pulled her closer, rimming her with his tongue.

Lena hummed around Mel's penis, enjoying the feeling when he jerked and groaned, so she did it again. Relaxing as much as she could, she released him and took him again, taking him farther this time. She could almost feel his head brushing her tonsils. She swallowed and he moaned her name, grabbing her hair and holding her head as he started thrusting in and out of her mouth.

Lena licked and sucked, trying to keep pace with his movements, but it was impossible. "Hold still and let him take you," R.J. instructed, stroking his own cock while he watched them.

Hal stopped what he was doing and began stroking himself, watching Mel's cock disappear in and out of Lena's mouth. He unconsciously timed his movements to match Mel's as he watched.

R.J.'s hand was also moving up and down, watching as Lena sucked and licked on Mel's monster of a cock. Seeing all that meat disappear inside a woman's mouth just did something for him.

Mel stopped and lifted Lena's mouth away from him. "I want to be inside you when I come, honey."

Hal released her hips and let Mel move her to straddle him, handing Mel a condom from the pile he had put beside the tub and grabbing a tube of lube.

Mel rolled the condom on then positioned Lena, draping her legs over his hips. R.J. moved around behind her and took the lube from Hal. "While Mel is fucking you, darling, I'll be stretching this little ass. Later tonight I will want to play more there."

Mel slowly started impaling Lena, leaning back against the side of the tub. At the same time, she felt a dribble of what she assumed was cold lube over her little round hole and felt not only it but her pussy clench. Hal slapped her sharply on one rear cheek. "Don't tense up, let them in," he said, rubbing his hand around her, soothing the place he had smacked.

Lena relaxed and R.J. slowly worked one finger inside her, easing inside her while Mel did the same with his cock in her pussy.

Hal knelt up beside her and told her, "Open for me, baby." When Lena opened her mouth, he slowly pushed his engorged cock past her lips and into her mouth.

Lena swirled her tongue around the head, licking and sucking. She didn't believe how sexy she felt with the three men loving her. It was the most erotic thing she had ever experienced to have all of them focusing on her.

R.J. added a second finger and thrust them slowly in and out of her ass, scissoring them to stretch her. He would use a plug later, but she wasn't ready for that yet.

Chapter Nine

Lena woke the next morning surrounded by the three men. She knew now why the tub, shower, and bed looked as if a football team could fit in them. By the time she and the three men were all together, it was nice and cozy.

After they finished in the tub, the men had taken Lena to the shower and quickly washed her before putting her to bed and crawling in with her.

She had slept the night through for the second night in a row. In her apartment, there was always some commotion and she got very little sleep. Feeling like a new woman, she snuck out of the bed and grabbed one of the men's shirts to put on. She was going to explore the kitchen and see if she could find something for breakfast. So far they had had all of their meals in the diner or delivered and she wanted to cook for them.

She managed to find everything she needed to make some Spanish omelets and started things cooking. She found coffee and made a pot, then went through the cabinets, making a list of things she would need to prepare meals. If she was going to stay, then she was going to make herself useful. She found everything she needed and started a batch of chocolate chip cookies. After putting the first pan of cookies in the oven, she sat and drank a cup of coffee, waiting for the men to wake up.

While she was drinking her coffee, she grabbed her phone to check her e-mail. She hadn't checked it since Thursday night and there were several. Looking through the list of notices she had, they were all either from prospective employers, friends, or junk, except one, which was titled "important." She didn't know the sender and almost deleted it without opening it, but decided to check it out in case it really was important.

She was just about to open it when Mel came walking around the corner. He wore a pair of jeans with the top button undone. "Good morning, beautiful. Something smells great."

Lena smiled and got up to pour him a cup of coffee. As she set it in front of him, he thanked her and said, "You don't have to wait on us. You're not here for that."

"I don't mind. I like to cook and didn't do much just for myself. It's fun." She pulled the cookies out of the oven and put them on a rack to cool. Then she turned and set the table for the four of them.

R.J and Hal joined them a few minutes after she had everything set out and they all sat to eat.

After breakfast, the men insisted on cleaning up since Lena had done the cooking and she went to dress while they did. Hal wanted to take her shopping while R.J. and Mel went to take care of some things at the office.

Hal insisted on taking her to buy some new things to wear in the office and he wanted her to have a few special things to wear for nights out and play evenings at home. They planned on taking her to Club de Fleurs one day soon and he wanted to get her some club wear. Before they left they promised R.J. and Mel a fashion show when they all returned later that evening.

Lena had forgotten all about the e-mail with the business of breakfast and then shopping until they got home later that afternoon. She might not have thought about it for a couple days except that her phone was sending off a low battery signal and she needed to charge it.

Taking her bags and phone back to the bedroom, she sat on the bed to plug it into the charger and look at the e-mail.

As she started to open the e-mail, she remembered she needed to call her parents. Even though they didn't get along very well she tried to call them every Sunday to make sure everything was okay.

It was the usual conversation about how well her brother was doing with the farm, how they wished she would come home, how they could use her help. Then the conversation turned to her social life. When she was getting married and so on. After catching up on all the town and family gossip with her mother, Lena finally hung up the phone and started to close her eyes when she remembered the e-mail.

Deciding not to put it off any longer, she opened the program and checked for anything new. There was one more from the same sender with the same title. Checking the time and date, she saw it had been sent while she had been fixing breakfast.

She chose to open the oldest one first. There was no message, only a picture of the dog she had left on the farm when she moved to the city. At first, she couldn't figure out why anyone would send her a picture of Duggy, her dog, until she noticed his lifeless eyes. Staring at the picture harder, she closed it and called her mom back.

Her mom apologized and said she had forgotten to tell her about Duggy, and that they had found him a few days earlier. The vet thought he had gotten into a poison of some kind. No one that her mother knew of had taken the picture or sent it to her. After Lena was done with the phone call, she opened the other e-mail. It was a picture of her dad and brother working with one of the animals. This one had a red X marked through her brother and the word "next" written in red ink underneath it.

She screamed and threw the phone down. Hal, Mel, and R.J. all came running into the room to see what was happening and she told them. Mel retrieved the phone from the floor—luckily it wasn't broken—and looked at both e-mails. A third one had arrived in the short time it had taken for her to call her mother and talk to the men.

Mel opened it and it was a short video of her and Hal in one of the shops they had gone to. This one was titled "We know."

Mel and R.J. both started making phone calls while Hal comforted Lena.

The first call Mel made was to Tucker Hague to apprise him of the situation. He knew Tucker was a good man and would do what was needed to keep Lena's family safe. Tucker already had men in place and would hire more if necessary. While Mel was on the phone with Tucker, R.J. called Lance Lewis with the updated information.

Phone calls handled, R.J. and Mel went back to join Hal with Lena and tell her what they had done.

Lena was crying softly and Hal was murmuring to her, reassuring her everything would be taken care of. "But what about Trina? She doesn't have any family here she can stay with. What's she going to do?" Lena started looking around for her phone. "I need to call her and tell her what's going on."

Mel and R.J. walked up as she was struggling with Hal, trying to convince him that she had to save everyone. "Lena, settle," R.J. said firmly and she relaxed somewhat.

Mel sat on the side of the bed. "Lena, we have people with your family and there are three brothers who were all Marines with Trina. They will move her to a safe house if they can't protect her at her house," he told her, taking one of her hands in his. "I will have them bring her by the office tomorrow so that you can see her."

"Oh, I can't go to the office with all this happening," Lena said.

"Yes, you can. You will be safest there and we can't stay home to watch you. You need to be where we can keep you safe and that is with us until we get it all figured out. So tomorrow you will put on one of the new outfits Hal bought you for the office and start your new job. I will arrange for the Lewis brothers to bring Trina in around lunch and we will all take you both to a nice long lunch. Okay?"

Going to work and keeping busy sounded better than sitting around and worrying all day. She did want to see Trina and find out about the Lewis brothers and how that was working out.

The rest of Sunday was quiet. The men kept Lena busy, but she knew something was bothering them because one of them was continually sneaking off to make a phone call or they were checking their phones for messages even though they tried not to let her know it.

Finally, she couldn't take it anymore and asked what was going on.

Hal took her by the hand and led her over to the sofa. All three men had been sitting at the table doing some paperwork while Lena watched a movie. "We have several teams working on finding out who has been sending you the e-mails and pictures. They have been reporting in and we are compiling all the information to see if we are getting anywhere," he explained to her.

"So have you found anything out?" Lena asked, wondering if she really wanted to know. She was afraid the answer wouldn't be good news.

"Nothing we didn't expect. We know more now than we did and have several teams that haven't reported in yet," Mel answered, walking over to join them. He sat on the couch beside Lena, putting his arm around her shoulders and pulling her close.

"How big is your agency? I mean, how many men do you have working for you? Is it a lot?" Lena was curious to find out more. Not only about the agency but about the men themselves.

"We have over one hundred people working for us. Most are agents in the field but you will eventually meet all of them as they come into the office. So far the three of us have been handling things, but we are growing and getting busier. We need someone pretty to greet people and answer the phones, help with filing, and maybe even take over the payroll eventually," R.J. explained, smiling.

"The business started growing very quickly and we are taking over some cases from a friend, Kyle Masters. He recently got married and is backing out of the business. He owns a fetish club we would like to take you to."

"Do you mean Kyle Masters, the former bodyguard who owns Club de Fleurs?" Lena asked excitedly.

"How do you know that?" Mel asked. Kyle and Jenna were very private people. The club was exclusive and not well known.

"Jenna is my cousin. I was at their wedding. I have lunch with her every couple of months. She will be so excited to hear I'm coming to the club. I have to call her and let her know. When will we go?" Lena answered, excited to be able to see her cousin.

Mel put one hand on her leg to slow her down as she wiggled nervously on the couch, ready to go call Jenna. "Honey, you need to wait until we figure out what's going on before you call anyone. We don't want any more people involved in this than we have to."

"Oh, yeah right. I'm sure Kyle would protect Jenna, but I don't want anything happening to her or their children. I'll wait to call her," Lena answered sadly.

"We are working on this as fast as we can. I'm sure we will have it all figured out soon. Do you want to have dinner here or go out? If we eat here we can either cook or order in. It's up to you," R.J. said, changing the topic.

They had dinner brought up. Then they all settled back to watch an action movie. The next day was Lena's first day working as a receptionist for the men. She was excited and nervous. She put on one of the new outfits Hal had bought for her and a pair of four-inch heels. She wasn't sure the shoes were office wear, but all three men promised they made her legs look a mile long and by their appreciative gazes she knew she looked good.

Mel tried to get her to leave her underwear off, but she refused. "Not in the office," she protested. He promised to rip them off her later and she just laughed, not believing him.

When they got to the office, Lena was surprised to see that the plain space that only had held a couch before now held a huge desk with a computer and phone and several chairs and several file cabinets.

"I know you only saw this space and R.J.'s office before, but let me show you around. We actually have the entire floor and can expand when we need to," Mel told her, taking her by the hand and leading her around.

"Hal has been primarily working out in the field and today will be his first day working in the office full-time. I also will be spending more time here in the office and will be interviewing some of the field staff to take on some of the duties Hal and I performed. When we decided to hire a receptionist we also decided to do some renovations to the office and start running it like the business it is. We can no longer handle things like we have in the past," Mel explained as he showed her his and Hal's office and the small kitchen they had.

After her tour, Mel took her back to the reception area and helped her get settled at her desk. After showing her how to work everything, he left her to get comfortable and went to his own office.

It didn't take Lena long to get settled and before she knew it, it was time for lunch. As promised, the men took her to meet with Trina and her security team at a restaurant.

"Wow, talk about hunkalicious, yum," Trina said when Lena introduced her to Mel, R.J., and Hal.

"Yeah, but the guys you're with aren't too hard on the eyes either," Lena responded, laughing and looking over at the table of six men.

The men had decided to let the girls have a table to themselves so they could talk, promising to stay close.

"Do you think all this is really necessary, Lena?" Trina asked, taking a sip of her margarita. The restaurant the men had taken them to served a wide variety of food and had a fully stocked bar, something the two girls planned on taking advantage of.

"I don't know," Lena answered Trina and went on to tell her all that had happened and why the men were so worried. "I guess, better safe than sorry, as they say," Lena said, finishing her story. "And I have to admit, the eye candy isn't bad. If all the field operatives look like our men, this will be a job worth keeping just for the view," Lena told her, laughing.

"Wait a minute, you might be comfortable with your men, but don't go calling Lance and his brothers mine. They are the bossiest most...most frustrating...guys I've ever met," Trina said, but while she was talking Lena couldn't help but notice that Trina kept looking over at the table where Lance and his brothers sat when they weren't looking at her. There was something there even if Trina didn't want to admit it.

Chapter Ten

The week progressed and Lena was slowly learning her job. She was more of an office manager than a receptionist. The men just didn't know it yet. She was taking over more and more of the administrative duties as time went on.

One week turned into two and nothing more had happened. Lena didn't receive any more e-mails and everything appeared quiet. The Lewis brothers brought Trina to see Lena at the penthouse a few times, but she still wasn't allowed to call anyone on her phone or even to have it. R.J. had taken charge of her phone and changed the passwords on all her accounts so she couldn't even get in and check her own e-mail. At two weeks it was annoying. By the third week of what she called imprisonment, she was getting sick of it.

"You don't let me contact anyone, you won't let me do anything but what you say. People in jail have more rights than I have," Lena told them one night when she had had enough. "I need to call my mother. I talk to her every week. She is going to be worried."

"We're trying to keep you safe," Mel said, and then he explained everything they were doing to accomplish this in detail.

Hal tried to explain why she needed to avoid contact with everyone who could reveal her location and distract her by taking her shopping again, but she still wasn't happy and they knew it.

Lena continued complaining and being bratty. She was worried and no matter what the men said they couldn't reassure her. Hal had the men with her family talk to her and let her know they were safe, but she was still not satisfied. Finally, Mel gave in and got a burner phone for her to call her mother on.

R.J. decided one night that they had all they were going to take from her. After Lena took a long, hot bath, the three men met her in the bedroom. They were all standing there in jeans and shirtless. Lena knew something was up. They didn't even allow her to get dressed before they led her down the hall to the playroom. "You've been acting bratty and we're all tired of it," R.J. said while he opened the door and let her in. Mel and Hal followed her.

There were dozens of scented candles lit all around the room. Hal guided Lena over to the spanking bench and helped her drape herself over it. "This is as much for you as it is for us. If any of it becomes too much, use the word 'red' and we will stop," Mel said from behind her.

"We think you need to come out of your head for a while. You've been thinking too much. We know you are starting to get frustrated. This will all be over soon. Until then we are just trying to keep you safe," Hal told her while he fastened fur-lined cuffs around both of her wrists and attached them to the hooks on the bench.

R.J. did the same with her ankles while Mel fastened a strap around her back. Once they were sure she couldn't move too much, they all started rubbing their hands all over her everywhere they could reach, stroking and soothing her, helping her to relax.

When Lena started to relax, R.J. stepped in front of her and opened his jeans. "I want you to take care of me while Hal and Mel focus on you," he told her, touching the small droplet of moisture at the slit of his penis to her lips.

Lena ran her tongue around her lips and opened her mouth for him. She felt something cool on her asshole and jerked. "Relax, it's just a little lube. You're ready for the biggest plug," Mel told her. She had been wearing a plug for a few hours after lunch each day at the office.

After lunch one of the men would take her into his office and play with her for a while before inserting the plug she was to wear that day. She would wear it until they took her home for the evening. Each plug was bigger than the last.

If this was the largest plug that could only mean that they all three planned on taking her together tonight. Lena felt her body quicken at the thought. They had taken her two at a time while the third one played with her ass but had not taken her all together even though she had begged and pleaded for them to do so.

She was glad it was finally going to happen. Something had been missing with the four of them and she hoped this was it. She felt the plug going in and tried to relax as much as she could. She couldn't be sure but she thought it was Hal slipping it inside her. It felt like his hands.

Once he finally got the plug seated it felt huge inside her and she knew it still wasn't as big as they were. Before she started wearing the plugs, they had shown her all of them so she would know how they progressed in size.

"Tonight we're going to add something, darling." It was Mel's voice that spoke from somewhere underneath her and she felt him sliding something into her pussy. "It's not as big as we are but it will help you get used to having something in both places. We have one more surprise."

Lena wondered what else they could have planned when she felt the plug in her ass start to vibrate. Shortly after it started the one in her pussy started vibrating, too.

R.J. grabbed her head with both hands and started thrusting slowly in and out of her mouth.

She was beginning to get used to everything that was happening when she felt hands rubbing and squeezing her ass. "Just warming you up a little," Hal said when he began lightly slapping each of her ass cheeks.

Lena was starting to relax into the feelings and let her mind drift when R.J. pulled away and started releasing her wrists. Someone was also releasing her ankles. The plug in her ass and vibrator in her pussy were taken out and she was lifted off of the bench. "We're going to move this over to the bed, honey," Mel told her as he settled her in his arms and carried her over to the bed where Hal was lying on his back in the center of the huge mattress.

"Baby, I want you to climb up there and mount Hal. He's all ready for you," Mel told her, putting her carefully on the bed.

Hal was lying there, his condom-covered cock pointing up like a flagpole. He held out his hands, reaching for her.

Lena crawled over to him. Hal placed a hand on each hip and guided her to straddle him, helping her sheath his rock-hard cock in her tight warm pussy.

As she slid down on him, she moaned and threw her head back, her hair brushing his thighs. Hal pulled her down until he was fully immersed inside her. He held her hips a minute, letting her adjust to his size and the position.

He pulled her down until she was lying on his chest with her ass in the air. "R.J.'s going to put some lube on you now. Relax."

Lena felt the cold drizzle of lube over her ass and then fingers working it in and around her little round hole. "Relax, this is going to be tight," R.J. told her, grasping one hip and fitting his cock to her. He started slowly pushing until he got past the ring of muscle, then he held himself still.

"Oh, it's too big. I can't," Lena panted, and a few tears streaked down her face.

"Easy, baby, easy. Take some deep breaths with me and let your body get used to it. You can do this," R.J. told her, reaching one arm around to finger her clit. He pressed his body against her back until she was breathing with him and he felt the tension release from her.

"Better now, honey?" R.J. asked, still rubbing small circles around her clit. He could feel a different kind of tension in her body now and knew she was ready for more.

"I'm going to start moving now. We'll go slow and let you get used to it at first," Hal told her, replacing R.J.'s hand on her hip with his and using it to guide her into the rhythm they wanted.

Mel had been watching Hal and R.J. get inside their girl and wasn't going to be left out. Crawling up beside her on his knees, he grasped her head with both hands. "I've got something for this pretty little mouth to do," he said, kissing her thoroughly.

When he released the kiss, Lena opened her mouth and let him feed himself inside her. All three of her men were loving her at once. The feelings were so intense.

R.J. squeezed her clit, drawing her attention back to him. "We're going to speed up now," he told her.

He and Hal set up a quick pace where when one was in the other was out. Mel quickly caught up to them and the three of them were thrusting rapidly in and out of her in a frenzy. The men came one after another.

Mel came first, pulling away and cradling her head against his thigh as he caught his breath. Then Hal came with a shudder beneath her, and finally R.J. behind her, falling on her and Hal.

Lena felt her body start to quicken and R.J. began pinching and pulling her clit to give her the push she needed. She felt the spasms go through her body and collapsed against Hal, the world going black.

The men quickly removed themselves from Lena and carefully carried her to the shower where all three of them gently washed her before carrying her to bed and tucking her between them.

"I've never seen that happen before. Do you think she's okay?" R.J. asked, brushing a lock of hair out of Lena's face.

"Yeah, we just wore her out, poor thing. She just needs some rest," Mel said, brushing a kiss along Lena's lips.

Lena woke the next morning and something had changed. She was in bed alone and didn't see any signs of her men. She grabbed the first shirt she found and walked out to the dining room where she found them all sitting at the table talking and drinking coffee.

She grabbed a cup and went to sit with them. Usually, one of them would grab her and pull her onto their lap or pull a chair for her to sit with them, but not today.

"What's going on?" she asked. She could tell by the disgruntled looks on their faces that something was up.

"How well do you know Greg Bates?" Mel asked, a very serious look on his face.

"He's Simon's uncle. I met him once while I was dating Simon," Lena answered, wondering what was going on.

"Are you sure you just met him the one time?" R.J. asked, pushing his chair away from the table and walking toward her.

"It might have been twice, why? What's up?" Lena was starting to get nervous. Something was wrong.

"Well, we were going through some of Simon's records looking for evidence and trying to find out who he was working for when we found this check made out to cash with your signature on it," Hal said, waving the copy of the check in her face.

"Oh, sometimes Simon had me write checks out of a loan account to pay expenses. That was probably for his lunch or something," Lena said, relaxing.

"Pretty expensive lunch, Lena. Look closer at the check. It's for ten thousand dollars and it's made out to Greg Bates. Why would Simon be giving his uncle that kind of money? Why did you sign the check?" Hal said, handing her the paper.

"That can't be right. I never signed anything that big. The account was small, only five thousand dollars, and was supposed to be used for Simon's expenses and any fees we needed to pay out of it. There's no way I signed a check for that amount." Lena was sure she'd never seen a check that big. But as she looked at it, it looked like her signature.

"Lena, there was close to two hundred fifty thousand dollars in that account. Do you know where it came from?" Mel asked her. All three men were standing towering over her, making her very nervous.

"No, no. That's not right. There's no way there was that much money in that account. You have the numbers wrong. Somebody made a mistake." Lena shook her head. This wasn't right. She might not have known everything that was going on but there was no way there was that kind of money in that account.

"Lena, somebody was writing the loan checks out of that account. We have checks here totaling over half a million dollars, all with your signature on them."

"No, I never signed checks for that amount. Anything over five hundred dollars had to go to Simon to sign. He was in charge of all of that," Lena protested.

"Not only do we have the checks you signed for Simon, but we found the same thing was happening at Franklin Franks' bank. You signed all of the checks. What kind of scam do you think you were pulling, lady?" Hal asked, grabbing her by the arm and pulling her to stand up against him.

"I never signed any checks like that at either bank. All the big checks had to be approved by a manager. I would never do anything like that." Lena couldn't believe what they were accusing her of.

"Lena, we found your account in the Cayman Islands. It has over two million dollars in it," Mel said.

"If I had two million dollars why would I be driving a death trap and living in a hovel? Huh? Tell me that, wise guys. I don't have that kind of money and never have. Somebody is trying to frame me. You knew that going in. You were the ones who told me that. You also told me you didn't believe that any of it was true. What changed all of a sudden?" Lena was furious. She thought they had believed that she had nothing to do with it and now look how they were acting.

"You could be hiding everything, saving it for your lover. How do we know you weren't involved in this from the beginning?" R.J. screamed at her. He walked up behind her, crowding her into Hal, and grabbed her shoulder, shaking her. "I was falling for your act, lady, and I use the word loosely. No lady I know could act the way you have. What kind of game are you playing? Don't think we won't find out."

He couldn't believe how she had duped them, all of them, but most of all him. He had been falling for her act. She had to have been in on it. All the evidence and paperwork pointed to her. How else could her signature have gotten on those checks? There was no way that much money passed through her hands without her knowing what was going on. No one was that naïve.

She tore her arm away from R.J. and pushed away from him. Shoving Mel and Hal out of her way, she ran back to the bedroom, slamming the door behind her. She ran into the closet and grabbed the first thing she could find to throw on. She'd go stay with Trina if they didn't want to believe her.

"You know she's right, Mel. She had no idea any of this was going on before we met her. Hell, she didn't even know someone was after her. As bad as all this looks, there has to be an explanation for it. We just have to dig deeper," Hal said, running his hand through his hair. He knew that despite all the evidence to the contrary there was no way Lena could have been involved to the extent of two million dollars. Mel's contact with the FBI had to be wrong. He grabbed his phone.

"I'm calling John. There has to be something they missed somewhere. I'm having him send everything to the office. We'll meet him and his team there. Then we will all sit and go over everything," Mel said, thinking about what Hal said. They needed to look into this deeper and be sure. Something had to be wrong somewhere.

"What about Lena? If we're all at the office working, who will be here with her?" Hal asked, finally pulling his head out of his ass and realizing just what they had done.

"We'll take her over to the safe house Lance and his brothers are watching Trina at. She can stay there until we figure this out," Mel said and started gathering the paperwork they had spread out all over the table and putting it in his briefcase.

"R.J., go get her packed up for a few days and I'll call the Lewis brothers and give them a heads-up," Hal said, helping Mel gather the paperwork.

R.J. nodded and headed for Lena's room. They were going to figure this out. Even if Lena had made a mistake, they would help her get it fixed. They would do whatever it took to get her out of this mess.

He couldn't wait to see the look on her face when he told her they were still willing to help her and that everything would be okay. She might have to serve a little time on probation, but that would be okay. Everyone had a past and made mistakes. This could still be fixed. He would have to punish her for her deception of course, but everything could be corrected.

Even though all the evidence pointed to her guilt, R.J. knew deep down that the woman who had stolen his heart couldn't have done what they accused her of knowingly. There had to be something, some way to get her out of this, and he was going to find it.

He marched down the hall and tried to push the door open. It was locked. "Lena, let me in," he said, knocking gently on the door. Nothing. He knocked again harder and called again for her to let him in, thinking maybe she was in the shower.

Hal and Mel heard him pounding on the door and demanding that she let him in or he was going to break it down. Hal grabbed the key from the kitchen and met Mel in the hall where he was trying to keep R.J. from breaking down the door.

"Here, move. I have the key," Hal said, shouldering R.J. out of the way and opening the door. "Lena, we need to talk."

He walked over to the bathroom, opening the door. Empty. Mel was already looking in the closet. She was gone.

"Did you hear her leave?" Mel asked. R.J. and Hal both shook their heads and went off to search the other rooms to make sure she wasn't hiding somewhere.

"She's not here. How did she get out without us hearing her?" Mel asked, pacing up and down the hall.

"She went down the emergency exit stairs in my room. I showed her the morning you two were acting like the assholes we all are and fighting in the living room. I didn't want her to see you two beating the shit out of each other and took her down the stairs to the elevator," Hal said, holding his head in his hands.

"Okay, where do you think she would go?" R.J. asked.

"She's cousins with Kyle's wife. She might go there. Maybe Trina knows more. She might head there, too. Have one of the Lewis brothers go to Trina's house in case she shows up there," Mel said, grabbing his keys and throwing Hal's to him. "R.J., you take Thurston and the car and start driving around in case she decided to go walk off her anger, but I think she ran."

"Got it. What are you two going to do?" R.J. asked, grabbing his phone to call Thurston and get the car.

"I'm going to the office. If she goes there I'll be waiting. Hal's heading to the safe house to talk to Trina and see if she knows of anywhere else Lena might go."

The three men separated to go hunt their woman.

LENA GRABBED HER PURSE, wishing she knew what the men had done with her phone but didn't dare take the time to look. She could call her mother and get the numbers she needed. If she couldn't stay with Jenna, Jenna would know of a place she could go.

When she was able to reach Jenna by phone and explain what was going on, Kyle, Jenna's husband, insisted that one of his men pick her up and take her somewhere safe until they could figure out what was going on. It was a better plan than the one Lena had, which so far had consisted of roaming the streets alternately crying and laughing out loud at her predicament. She was surprised the men in the little white coats hadn't come after her already.

A black SUV pulled up in front of the doorway she was standing in and a tall man with black hair jumped out and walked up to her. "Are you Lena? I'm Jarrod, Kyle sent me. Come on. I'm to take you to his house and we'll talk there. On the ride, you can tell me what's going on."

Lena told Jarrod her story as they drove. "Oh, I know those three. They are members of the club and Kyle works with them occasionally," he told her as they pulled in front of a huge house.

Jenna ran out and greeted her, pulling her in the house and up the stairs. "Come on, I have the kids busy playing for now. We called the sitter to help for a while so you and I can talk then we will meet with Kyle and make a plan. I swear the man is not happy unless he has a plan."

Jenna had some clothes Lena could wear and they got her set up in the spare room until they could decide what their next move would be. "I can't stay here forever. I need to find a job and a place to live. I guess I need to start over." Lena's voice broke as she said that last part, realizing what all she was giving up. In one hour she'd lost her job, place she lived, and the three men she loved most in her life. She didn't even know where they had stashed her car. She had nothing.

"Don't worry about any of that yet. Kyle will figure something out. He's good at that. We can always use a backup receptionist or bartender at the club. Melissa is just part-time behind the bar and some nights it's a lot for Jarrod to handle on his own. Kyle and I will take care of you," Jenna told her, giving her a big hug. "Come on, let's check on the kids and see how they are doing. Then we will go find Kyle and see if he knows anything more."

"You don't think he called Mel and the guys, do you?" Lena wasn't ready for them to know where she was.

"Honey, I've been with you and I don't know what Kyle did." Jenna wasn't going to tell her that she was sure Kyle had called Mel, R.J., and Hal and let them know how stupid they were being. Lena didn't need to hear that yet.

Chapter Eleven

Lena spent two weeks moping around Jenna's house. She helped her with the children and helped Kyle track down who could be framing her and why.

Every time the phone or doorbell rang, she jumped, hoping her men had come to their senses and were there to apologize and take her back. That was when she wasn't so mad she was plotting how to make them all pay, if she ever talked to them again.

She knew Kyle had been talking to them. She had walked into his office once and was sure she had heard Mel's voice on the speakerphone. Kyle had quickly picked up the receiver then pointedly glared at her until she left his office. He kept the door locked from then on and she was sure she had heard him telling Jenna that she was going to get ten swats for not keeping a better eye on Lena. She didn't know if Jenna got in trouble or not, but Jenna was very happy the next day.

After the third week of watching Lena mope around the house, Jenna couldn't take it anymore and decided to talk to Kyle. Normally she tried to stay out of his business, but this involved her family too.

"We have to do something about Lena. I can't stand seeing her like this," Jenna said when Kyle let her into his office, locking the door behind him. Jenna knew about Lena walking in and understood why he didn't want it happening again.

He pushed his chair back and pulled her into his lap. "I know, baby. I don't like seeing her hurting either. I can tell you that R.J., Hal, and Mel realize what a mistake they have made and are close to solving this with the help of Mel's contacts at the FBI."

"Do they have a plan to get Lena back?" Jenna wanted everyone to be as happy as she and Kyle were.

"No, but I do," Kyle said and told her what he had planned and how she was going to help.

Mel, Hal, and R.J. had pulled every string they could and had Kyle pull a few, too, until they managed to find out who was after Lena and why they had picked her. They weren't going to quit until they had her completely exonerated.

Mel knew what he and his FBI contact had found was just the tip of the iceberg, but they didn't know until they dug further just how deep the threat ran. It wasn't just mob contacts. Simon's Uncle Greg had been using the bank to launder drug money and then used it to support the campaigns of several high-ranking officials in the local government. It was quite the hornets' nest they had opened and a mess that could take years to untangle to its fullest extent. They had no idea how far-reaching the ramifications could be. Simon and Frank were low men on the totem pole and Lena was just a pawn in their game.

After weeks of work, Mel, Hal, and R.J. had convinced Mel's contact with the FBI that Lena knew nothing and they had found the evidence they needed to not only convict Frank and Simon, but Simon's Uncle Greg also. It also looked like a few members of Congress would have some questions to answer.

With Frank and Simon both in jail, the groups that had been targeting Lena realized that she was innocent and the threats to her were withdrawn. Mel got an anonymous message that simply said, "the girl is safe," and nothing more happened. It was over.

The threat to Lena cleared, it was time for the men to get their woman back. If she would take them.

When Kyle had told Jenna he had a plan, it meant he did. Getting everything to fall into place was the easy part. Kyle's plans rarely failed.

Kyle arranged for Lena to take some bartending shifts with Jarrod at the club to "help out" for a couple days and made sure that Mel, Hal, and R.J. were meeting him at the club one of those nights.

Jenna loaned Lena one of the outfits Kyle had bought her for the club, convincing her it was appropriate to wear since she was tending bar. Everything set up, Kyle and Jenna sat back to watch the show.

Chapter Twelve

Jarrod was great to work with. He was good looking and sexy. If she hadn't already fallen head over heels for Mel, R.J., and Hal, Lena could see herself having a good time with Jarrod. This was the third night she had helped out at the bar and she was getting comfortable with him. He was sweet, a big flirt, and a teddy bear. Very protective of her. On her first night working the bar, one of the regulars had gotten a little handsy and Jarrod had explained to him in no uncertain terms that Lena was not available to play.

The second night after they had everything cleaned up, Jarrod offered to do a scene with her, but she refused. She didn't want anyone but her men.

The third night Lena worked was the busiest and she didn't have time to stop between serving drinks. Kyle had invited some of his friends from another club to do a wax demonstration and the club was crowded with people who had come to watch it. It was busy enough that Kyle had called Melissa, the part-time bartender, in to help. Watching them together, Lena could tell there was something between Jarrod and Melissa but she wasn't sure what was going on with them.

It was busy enough that she really didn't have time to pay a lot of attention to what was going on. Jarrod and Melissa were handling the customers at the bar, and Lena was busy filling drinks for the waitress and helping wait tables when needed.

After the first demo was over and things were starting to quiet down, several of the waitresses went on break, leaving Lena to wait on tables.

Lots of people had left after the demo and only a few tables were occupied. One table was back in a dark corner and although Lena couldn't make out the faces she knew there were people back there.

"I'm grabbing this last table, then I'm taking a break if you're good with that?" she called to Jarrod and Melissa, and ventured back to take the order. One of the lights must have been out because the corner was darker than normal.

Knowing she would be safe in the club she walked on back to the corner when someone grabbed her around the waist and put a hand over her mouth. "Don't fight, baby, it's just us," Mel's voice said in her ear.

Lena sagged in relief at first then she got mad. Kicking and struggling, she was carried off to one of the private rooms. "We want to talk to you," Hal said when Mel let her go, locking the door behind him.

"Well I don't want to talk to you," Lena answered, turning to storm out the door.

R.J. blocked her path, putting his back to the door and blocking her way.

"Lena, we're sorry. We looked at the evidence and didn't dig any deeper," Hal said, starting to explain. "We've spent the last month going through things and talking to people to clear you. We had to get to the bottom of what was going on and make sure the people who had caused this were punished."

"Well, I'm glad you did that. I've been cleared of everything then?" Lena asked, her voice full of relief. She had been worried about going to jail and endangering Jenna, Kyle, and their family. She was glad that part of it was over. "If that's what you needed to tell me, you didn't have to come here to do it. You could have gotten a message to me through Kyle. I need to go back to my job now." Lena tried to push R.J. out of the way and go out the door.

"Honey, we were fools. We shouldn't have gone off on you the way we did. You were right. We knew better and just let our emotions take over. We should have trusted you," Mel said, walking up behind her and slipping his arms around her.

Lena twisted out of his arms and stepped away from him. "I'm glad you realized your mistake, but I really need to go now. Jarrod and Melissa might need my help." She really wanted to get away from them and think. Part of her was still hurt from the way they had acted. She really wanted to give in and just let them hold her, but it wasn't going to be that easy.

"Please let me go," she said, turning to look at Hal, silently pleading for his help.

"Lena, please just listen to us. We really are sorry and we want you to come back," R.J. said, laying both of his hands on each of her shoulders and turning her toward him.

"Guys, I need time to think. I won't lie to you, I was really hurt by the way you acted. Then you didn't contact me for almost a month and show up here tonight expecting me to forgive you. Really?" They really didn't expect her to give in just like that, did they?

"Please let me get back to work. I owe Kyle and Jenna for letting me stay with them for so long. I'll talk to you later," Lena said when R.J. finally moved and opened the door for her.

Lena practically ran back to the bar. She really wanted to just give in and let her men hold and comfort her but couldn't let go of the way they had behaved. How did she know that they wouldn't act like that again if something else came up? They hadn't trusted her. Now they expected her to forgive everything and go back to the way things were. She wasn't sure she could.

Melissa and Jarrod could tell something was up, but the next demo was due to start soon and traffic was picking up at the bar. They were getting busy again. Lena didn't have time to stop for a breath, let alone think, which was a good thing. When things calmed down and she could take another break, the table her men had been at was empty. She did a quick walk around the bar but didn't see any signs of them. She was glad they had listened to her and were giving her some space in one way, but disappointed, too, that they had apparently given up so easy.

Things were starting to quiet down, so Jarrod told her that he and Melissa could handle the rest of the evening and clean up. Lena really didn't want to go back to Jenna's and face Jenna's questions so she roamed around watching some of the scenes for a while before making her way back to the bar. "Not ready to go yet?" Melissa asked, setting a bottle of water in front of her.

"I'm not sure what I want to do," Lena answered her, taking the bottle of water and rolling it around in her hands. "I want to go back but I'm not sure they won't hurt me again." She had talked with Melissa one night and told her everything that had happened. She needed a neutral ear and Jenna wasn't it.

"Honey, what you need to ask yourself is, do you love them? If the answer is yes, you will know what to do. We all make mistakes and we try to learn from them. Don't let this mistake ruin your life. If you don't give them a chance you will regret it for the rest of your life." Melissa sounded like she knew what she was talking about. Lena could tell that Melissa had made a decision with what she had said. After she finished talking to Lena, Melissa walked over to Jarrod and put her arms around him, whispering something in his ear. Maybe Melissa was taking her own advice.

Lena finished her bottle of water and then grabbed her coat. Kyle and Jenna had loaned her a car to get back and forth from the club, so she didn't need to wait for a ride.

When she walked out to the parking lot, there were Mel, Hal, and R.J. all standing beside her car. "How long were you going to wait?" she asked, walking up to the car and hitting the remote to open the doors.

"As long as it took," R.J. answered, opening the driver's door for her.

"We'll follow you back to Kyle's to make sure you're safe," Mel said, leaning in the passenger door and making sure she was belted in and safe.

"You don't need to follow..." Lena started to say but could tell it was useless. They would follow her regardless.

When they got to Kyle and Jenna's the lights were on and Lena could tell Jenna had waited up for her. She waited for the men to pull up behind her before getting out. Hal was there to help her out of the SUV and all three men walked her to the door.

"Thank you for following me and walking me to the door. Um...well...good night, I guess." Lena didn't really want to let them leave, but knowing Jenna was waiting up she didn't want to invite them in.

"Can we call you?" R.J. asked, looking nervous.

"Yeah, I never got a cell phone. You will have to call on Kyle and Jenna's phone," Lena answered.

"We will call you tomorrow, beautiful. Get a good night's sleep," Mel said, pulling her into his arms and brushing her mouth with his in a gentle "I'm sorry" kiss.

Mel handed her to Hal, who threaded his hand through her hair before taking his own kiss. "Good night, baby, I love you," he said as he turned her over to R.J.

R.J. took her in his arms and backed her up against the door, kissing her so thoroughly that her toes curled. "I love you, too, Lena, come back to us," he said, letting her go and walking away.

Lena let herself in the house and closed the door, locking it behind her and setting the alarm. Leaning against the door, she stood for a minute, thinking about the three men and their behavior. Maybe she should give them a second chance.

"Hey, how are you doing?" Jenna said quietly, walking up and putting her hand on Lena's shoulder.

"I'm good. Tired. It was busy tonight. I think I'm going to bed," Lena answered her and walked away. Lena knew she was being rude and that Jenna had stayed up to talk to her, but she couldn't do it. She needed some time alone to think.

As she walked to her room, she saw Kyle exiting the room at the end of the hall. The door had always been locked and she wasn't sure what was in there. When she had asked Jenna, she had told her that was a room they didn't want the kids in and nothing more.

A few minutes later she heard Jenna giggling and the low timbre of Kyle's voice and then a door opening and closing. It must have been the one at the end of the hall, because it sounded too far away to be their bedroom door which was across the hall from Lena's.

The next morning, it was very late before Jenna came down. Lena had already had breakfast, and she and the nanny had fed and bathed the children. Emma, the nanny, had already taken the children off to the park.

Jenna was walking stiffly but had a smile on her face and a dreamy look in her eyes. Lena didn't pry but was glad Jenna looked happy. When Kyle came out of his office for lunch, he had a satisfied grin on his face that explained everything.

Later that afternoon the doorbell rang, a messenger with flowers for Lena from all three of her men. That evening they each called her and she talked for several hours with them, finally getting off the phone, not wanting to tie up Jenna and Kyle's line any longer.

The next day, Lena received a cell phone. R.J. called and explained that they wanted to be able to call and text her anytime and not have to depend on Kyle and Jenna to get through to her.

Gifts, texts, and calls continued through the week with the men begging her to come home or to go out with them. Friday arrived and Lena was scheduled to work at the club. The car she had been borrowing wasn't available that night, so she rode with Jarrod to the club.

The night was a busy one again and Lena didn't notice when her men came in the bar. By the time she was able to take a break most of the people had left for the evening. She, Jarrod, and Melissa worked hard getting everything cleaned up and getting ready to close the club down after the busy evening. Every night someone had to check the private rooms and make sure the ones that hadn't been rented for the evening were empty. Tonight it was Lena's turn. She grabbed the keys and started knocking on doors and opening them to make sure they were empty. She had checked all but one and after knocking let herself in to check and make sure it was empty.

She closed the door and turned to check the bathroom when the lights went out. Crap. Jarrod must not realize she was still in the rooms and the doors locked electronically so she was stuck until someone missed her.

She stood in the middle of the room and tried to remember the orientation so she could find a place to sit. She took a step into the room and was sure she heard something. Reaching out a hand she felt around, trying to find the couch or a chair somewhere to sit other than the floor.

Jumping at every little sound, she bent at the waist and reached out for the chair, trying to convince herself that Jarrod or Melissa would be in to find her shortly. *Relax, deep breath, relax,* she kept repeating to herself over and over. Mumbling the words, she inched forward, reaching for the chair until she felt the arm. She groped and felt until she was sure she had herself turned right and would sit in the chair instead of plopping on the floor. She eased herself down and as she got about halfway down, she felt someone or something grab her around the waist and pull her back. Letting out a scream, she reached around, swinging her arms and kicking her legs, and screaming as loud as she could.

A hand closed over her mouth and she was held in a tight grip. "Lena, stop!" she heard a firm voice say.

Slowly she stopped fighting and relaxed. Hal. She would know that voice anywhere. The hand was removed from her mouth and the arms around her lessened their tight grip.

"Okay now, baby?" That was R.J. He was the one holding her.

"Mel, are you here, too?" she asked the air, still unable to see anything.

"Yeah, just a minute, honey and I'll get the lights back on," he answered, and then the lights came on.

"Jeez, you guys scared the crap out of me. You're a bunch of assholes," she said, totally relaxing in R.J.'s lap. "Did you have to do all this? All you had to do was ask and I'd have come back here with you."

"How did we know that? We've been begging all week for you to meet with us and all you've done is put us off," Mel answered her, moving to sit on the arm of the chair she and R.J. were in.

Hal was standing in front of her, his arms crossed over his massive chest, looking down at her. He dropped to one knee and took her hand. "We couldn't take the chance you would put us off again," he told her, pulling her hand to his mouth and kissing each of her fingers.

R.J. moved his hands from her waist and cupped the undersides of her breasts. "Honey, we want you. We don't know how to say we're sorry differently. Haven't you punished us enough?" he asked, pulling her tank top up and sliding his hand up her bare stomach to the front clasp of her bra.

Lena really was happy to see them. They had been trying to make it up to her all week and she had planned on giving in on Sunday and going to see them. She just hadn't told them yet.

"Please, darling, say you'll come back home," Mel said, reaching for the hem of her very short skirt and pushing it up to reveal her thong.

She let her head fall back on R.J.'s shoulder, totally relaxing her body. "Yes, I'll come back," she told them, allowing her eyes to fill with tears. "I forgive you and understand why you did what you did." She felt R.J.'s tense body relax beneath her.

Mel leaned over and framed her face with both his hands, pulling her to him. "Thank you. You'll never regret this," he told her, pressing his lips to her and taking her mouth with his, staking his claim.

When Mel released her, Hal took his place, nibbling at her lips and pulling her up to lean against him. While she was standing, R.J. reached up and pulled her micro skirt and thong down her legs. Hal held her while she stepped out of them.

Hal set her back in R.J.'s lap, lifting her tank top and bra over her head, leaving her naked.

He spread her legs on the outside of R.J. and Mel knelt between them. "We have one thing we want you to wear and never take off," he said, pulling a box out of his pocket and opening it to reveal the largest chocolate diamond she had ever seen. "Will you marry us, Lena?" he asked, taking the ring out of the box and sliding it on her finger.

"Yes, yes, yes," she answered, tears running down her face. They all kissed her again and she gazed at the ring. "Tell me one thing?" she asked.

"What, baby?" Hal answered.

"What's R.J. stand for?" she asked and they all laughed.

"Richard James Blackmore," he answered. "Why?"

"Well, when I yell at you, and I'm sure I will, I want to be able to call you by your whole name," she answered, laughing. They all laughed.

R.J. lifted her and flipped her over his lap. "What are you doing?" she screamed, laughing harder.

"Showing you what I'll do when you yell at me," he said, and began smacking her ass with the flat of his hand.

Don't miss out!

Visit the website below and you can sign up to receive emails whenever Rose Nickol publishes a new book. There's no charge and no obligation.

https://books2read.com/r/B-A-QFBG-HRCJC

BOOKS 2 READ

Connecting independent readers to independent writers.

Also by Rose Nickol

All the President's Men
Derek's Darling Damsel
Tyler's Tasty Treat
Dillion's Dainty Delight

Ashcroft Security
Ashcroft Security Saving Lena

Club de Fleur
Club de Fleurs 3: Theresa`
Club de Fleurs 4: Rachel
Club de Fleurs 5: Tina's Twins
Club de Fleurs 2 Sadie
Club de Fleurs Tasha
Club de Fleur Melissa

Club de Fleurs
Club de Fleurs: Jenna

Men in Blue
Men in Blue Gavin's Bliss
Men in Blue Cara's Truth

Satan's Bears
Satan's Bears Saving Jasmine

Standalone
Kodiak Matings Bearly Mated
Jakey's Gift

Watch for more at rosenickol.com.

About the Author

Rose started writing professionally four years ago. Since then she's published more than twenty books. She now lives in Florida with her daughter, one cat and one dog.

Read more at rosenickol.com.

www.ingramcontent.com/pod-product-compliance
Lightning Source LLC
Chambersburg PA
CBHW031426150726
47989CB00002B/816